ON THE L___

by

Joy Burnett

License Notes

Acknowledgements

Thanks to my many friends who have read and reviewed this my first book, 'On The Loose', especially Andrew, Teresa, Lynne and Mark, and special thanks to Morgen Bailey who advised, encouraged and helped edit this book for me.

About the Book

Have you ever wondered what it's like to be forty and 'on the loose' after nearly twenty-three years of marriage? In my whole adult life I had been in just one relationship. Never been out, dated or had sex with anyone else, except my childhood sweetheart who turned into boring Brian, my shit of a husband. He ran off with a 'Miss Norway' look-alike and there I was, uninitiated in either the art of flirting or a satisfying sex life and no idea where to start.

'Get on the dating sites,' advised my best mate Teresa who had the social life of an eighteen-year-old even though she had a lazy beanpole of a son and a slightly dotty mother to take care of. 'Everyone is doing it.'

Mmmmmm, well... that started an interesting journey for me. I never appreciated that I had a sex drive or that there could be so many variations of a theme!

CHAPTER 1

As I stepped away from the bed, I suddenly caught sight of myself in the mirror. Not bad, I thought, for a forty two year old. I liked what I saw, and realised the soft glow on my skin and the sparkle in my eyes was due to the glorious sex I had just had with Tony. My hair was tousled and I had a distinct upward curve on my kiss-reddened lips. My breasts were still wet and sticky from his kisses and the champagne he had poured over them and my nipples still tingled from his tongue and teeth.

What an inventive lover he was turning out to be. He used his beautiful hands to caress and pleasure my body as if he was playing a piece of music, and I was learning how to tease and excite him too.

He had taken me along pathways I have never previously explored. How different I am now, I hardly recognise myself. Tony is the youngest of my lovers so far. I think he is number five or six. It's amazing what two years 'on the loose' can do for a girl.

***

Late in the afternoon in the early spring of 2002, I received a phone call that was to change my life and my whole perception of love, attraction and sex. The sun was shining in through the tiny hall window, making patterns on the dusky orange carpet and my little pale tabby cat Flo was curled up, taking a nap on the hall windowsill when the phone rang. Slightly miffed at her rest being disturbed, she mewed, stretched and jumped down as I walked into the hall and picked up the phone.

"Hello...Who?... What do you mean?"

The stranger on the other end of the phone told me his name and why he was calling. I caught my breath as I realised what he was saying. My husband was having an affair with his wife, and did I know, and what was I going to do about it? I realised I wasn't breathing and tried to take a breath which ended in a gulp, and I could feel my face crumpling and tears rushing into my eyes. I cleared my throat and tried to answer but the tone of my voice sounded clipped and strained.

"For how long?" I spluttered as I sat down on the bottom step of the stairs. "You know this for certain? No... no, I didn't, and how long did you say? Yes I will, I'll have to talk to him... absolutely not. Give me your number then." I took a deep shuddering breath and wrote down his name and number on the pad. When the call ended, I put my head in my hands and wept.

Six months later, I had come to terms with the fact that my husband had been seeing someone else for two years and was planning to tell me, but the 'someone else's' husband found out first and he had forced a showdown. The lady in question, Sophie, looked like someone out of a Norse legend; tall, blonde, slim and perfectly toned, with creamy gold skin. No kids, therefore no stretch marks or saggy boobs, and she and my husband just upped and offed together and are now living somewhere in Surrey.

I'd done with crying and hating him, changing the locks, sorting out his things, and being bitter and angry. Twenty-three years of marriage and he had left without a backward glance, or the least idea of how it tore my heart to see him go.

In the July, my forty-first birthday came and went. I drank a whole bottle of Chardonnay that day and felt terrible the next. I was throwing up and crying, and feeling sorry for myself when Brian had phoned and told me that he'd continue to pay the mortgage on the house, on condition I supported myself. He made it absolutely clear he wasn't going to provide anything more. It seemed a bit harsh and I shouted my misery down the phone at him.

Afterwards, as I began to feel better, I realised I was lucky. I had a lovely house in Stokesley, an exceptionally good village. If he continued to pay the mortgage, I could get another better-paid job to support myself. I made up my mind that I still had a few good years in me yet. I was healthy and capable of working so he could go fuck himself.

I was by now sexually frustrated, felt rejected and unloved. I missed the warmth of Brian's body and even the rather unsatisfying lovemaking. It's a complicated business between sex and love; where do they meet or separate? I had loved Brian since sixth form, or at least had thought I had, and other than a quick fumble with an oversexed co-worker at my first Christmas party in the office of Kenton's, I had never experienced another man.

I know that with a couple of nimble fingers and a bit of fantasy, I could easily arrive at orgasm considerably sweeter than the hurried, rather sweaty orgasms with Brian. Nevertheless, I'd thought that we had a good marriage; we enjoyed the same things, had two lovely sons and many mutual friends. I thought he was a man of honour. Instead he turned out to be a lying, cheating bastard. At that time I thought I'd never be able to trust another man again.

On a bright, sunny Sunday afternoon, my friend Tally arrived with a big box of my favourite chocolates and plenty of good advice. We sat drinking cappuccinos in the garden whilst chatting about the local gossip, and then I told her how Little Cock Brian was being a pain about money, and how I couldn't talk to him without losing it and crying. It somehow helped calling him Little Cock. I don't know why, ridiculous really as I had little or nothing to compare to.

Tally was sympathetic, and listened while I prattled on about the underpaid job I was doing and how unappreciated I felt -- da di da di da... It's wonderful having woman friends, they let you talk. They turn up with chocolates, wine or tissues the minute relationships go wrong, and offer completely biased sympathy such as, 'he wasn't worth it you know,' or, 'always was up his own backside,' and gleefully pick over why you are better off without him. True to form, Tally said, "You haven't been happy together for a long time, Laura. You'll soon find someone else."

7

"When do I ever get to meet a man? All I do is work and shop and mow the lawn. Not much fun there."

She, on the other hand, had a much more interesting tale to tell as she was deeply into an apparently fabulously sexual relationship with Mark who was at least ten years younger than she was, not very bright, but with a body like Adonis.

Tally and I had been friends for years and she was an integral part of my life, bringing her youthful optimism and wit into my sometimes-dreary and dull married life. She is more than ten years younger than me, crazy and beautiful, with a curvy body and long, glossy dark hair that swings as she moves. She flicked it back as she laughed. "He's doing me a power of good. You know what rotters I have managed to get involved with before. This is *just* sex and it really *is* fun, Laura."

Tally is so good-natured and generous that men have taken advantage of her. She has a thriving business designing rooms for hotels and is making more money than most of the men she has been seeing over the past couple of years. She oozes good energy and always smells of roses. Leaning over, she tickled Flo behind her ear, setting off a rumbling purr from my satisfied cat.

"Doesn't it bother you that Mark is so under endowed intellectually and mentally?" I had asked.

"Not a bit darling. I like him. He's a sweetie… No, it doesn't bother me one bit."

Smiling, I said, "Don't you need, you know, love and attention and someone to talk to, even if it is after... wouldn't you rather have someone with a bit more... *intellect?*"

"Oh," Tally said, screwing up her nose and closing her eyes in mock disdain. "I get plenty of attention and I've done the love bit, remember. If you can find me someone with a good body *and* a bit of intellect, that is also interesting as well, go ahead. I think it's impossible to get everything in one package. Just look at my track record. In the past four years I've had three relationships plus a few one-night stands, and did one of them have much to offer? Nooo…

They are either sexy *or* interesting, never both, and right now I want sexy and a bit of fun." She thought for a moment. "You know all my friends have settled for tolerable sex in exchange for babies, security, familiarity, occasional conversation… and from what I hear, it is *occasional…* plus an acceptable social life, but not one of them is having as much fun as I'm having with Mark." She looked thoughtful. "He's so good looking." Then she laughed. "And he takes his washing home to his mum... Oh sorry darling, did that hit a nerve?" she asked, looking at my stricken face. "I didn't mean you."

Isn't that exactly what I had done with Brian? It was as if she was talking about me.

"You're right of course, the sex was only occasional." I screwed up my face and grinned. "In fact, barely tolerable sometimes, but our social life has been good. Conversation practically stopped when Joe was born. Fun? No, not much of that."

I guess I'm really a typical example of an unfulfilled woman who settled for a nice man for comfort and support and children. There have been many times when I'd been aware that our marriage was not really good, and I had often wondered if this was normal. I'd never let my expectations get out of hand and tolerated Brian's moods and selfishness, telling myself I was lucky to have such a good, hardworking husband and two lovely, healthy sons.

It would be nearly two years later that I would be able to relate to Tally and her toy-boy and the fun they were having.

"So, tell me more Tally," I had asked.

"Well, Mark is very lively," she said with a twinkle. "He calls his cock his 'fruity rooty'.

Really, I know men have some odd names for the thing that dangles between their legs but 'fruity rooty?" Glory be. I laughed so much my mascara had ran down my face in sooty streams.

"He really is still just a kid but his 'fruity rooty' is all grown up, it just keeps going and going." She giggled. I dabbed at my messy make-up and hoped Tally would stay a bit longer and tell me more. "I'm just having a good time you know, and you should be doing the same instead of letting Brian get at you. He is just a sad old prick. He's never really been right for you and you're still young Laura," Tally said, "and incredibly good-looking. You could have any man you choose. You're so nice too, Laura. 'Gather ye rosebuds while you may' and all that."

"Thanks, Tal. Brian always said I was 'nice'. 'You're a nice woman Laura,' he'd say. "What does that mean? I don't think he would say that about Sophie, more likely 'you're a glorious, wanton sex kitten.' It's always 'nice' people who get dumped," I moaned. "For me, even chatting with men feels like an implicit act of faithlessness. I do meet a few men but not many, and I *am* flattered if *occasionally* I get chatted up, but I find it hard to go any further. I never have, you know… all the time I have been married. I've never considered adultery within the normal range of behaviour for bored women, as *some* of my friends seem to. I'm not sure that I'm prepared to have a relationship yet, and I don't want just a quick fuck."

Tally laughed. "You should, a quick fuck would cheer you up a bit, I'm sure. Get rid of the guilt and have some commitment-free sex." She tossed her gorgeous mop of dark curly hair back from her face; a throwback to her Greek grandmother, picked up her Gucci handbag and as she walked to the door, she said, "No, I like 'em young – young sweet guys with no imagination beyond their dicks. I have a good time – fun is what it's about darling, not his IQ. See you soon."

She kissed me affectionately and although I laughed at Tally's scepticism, I knew and understood that at thirty-plus years old she was beginning to fear her biological clock ticking away. I know that she really wanted a family and would make a wonderful mother. I raised a hand and waved her off as she sped away, music playing, hair flying, in her new sporty TT.

10

Tallulah Blake is one of the most beautiful young women I've ever known. She attracts men like fleas to a mangy dog, and has had her fair share of eligible men in the years I've known her. Unfortunately not one of them had treated her as she deserved, usually taking advantage of her good nature and generosity, or failing to make a positive commitment to her. Her one long-term relationship, with John, had ended bitterly after Tally had funded yet another of his business ventures which had failed miserably, basically because John was incapable of doing a full day's work. He took advantage of her again and again, and always promised that the next deal or business was the one that would keep them in style for the rest of their lives and enable Tally to cut her work commitments and have a family. Luckily, Tally was an independent and clever businesswoman and her art and design company flourished.

Here she was having an affair with handsome, baby-faced Mark. His use of language made him sound like a candidate from 'Pop Idol' or 'Big Brother'. He calls himself Markie for goodness sake, and used words like 'swinging,' 'hip' and 'cool' and calls his penis 'fruity rooty'!

It does make me wonder about my own sons, now twenty-three and eighteen. Perhaps they have it off with older women, using them to gather experience and the pleasure they can give? One never thinks of one's own children gathering sexual experience with older partners. Ah well, I'd probably never know about that!

So Tally had decided just to have some fun; perhaps I should do the same. I had been married for far too long and found it difficult to flirt at all with other men, but was flattered by the occasional attempted chat-up even though I couldn't ever think of anything funny or clever to say. I never took any of them seriously. Brian had been the only man in my life.

Later, after Tally had left, I got out of the shower and walked into the spare bedroom. I stood in front of the full-length mirror and watched myself rubbing my wet hair. When was the last time I looked at myself naked and without make-up? I tried to imagine if I were unfamiliar with the body I was looking at, whether it would seem attractive. I narrowed my eyes and turned slowly from side to side. I tried to see what Brian would have seen and why he had grown tired of me. I'm still in reasonably good shape, fairly slim, my breasts are large and firm and my skin is creamy and smooth except for some softness and wispy stretch marks on my lower abdomen. I have pretty feet too and my dark brown hair looks healthy and lustrous.

I suppose it happens to all married people after a few years together and children and all that; you just become part of the landscape, something you hardly notice until things start going wrong. I know that our lives had changed so much since we had the children, and his attention turned increasingly to his business and mine had been on the babies and not him. Maybe that is why he found somebody else more enticing. I tried to remember how it was when we first made love, how we first saw each other and I couldn't, I simply couldn't remember the first time at all, even though I had thought it was exciting and wonderful. No memory of any details and yet I can remember the film we saw and the thrill of his kisses. We were kids, what did we know about life? We were so inexperienced and I realise now that deep down I had felt resentful for years that life was passing me by without any real passion or thrills in it. Really without any fun or real love.

When we married, all our friends were doing the same. Our parents expected it of us. It was just the next step. It wasn't his fault and I wasn't unhappy. I'm sure he must have felt the same way.

I ran my fingers between my legs and touched my clitoris, aware that Brian had only ever rubbed it as if he was cleaning a spot off the car bonnet, and as I stroked myself, I yearned for a tender lover who could bring me to orgasm slowly and expertly. I longed for a little gentleness and sensuality, a slower, more loving, easier journey to the ultimate of pleasures. I'm sure that the art of good lovemaking is a desire to please and be pleased, and to experience joy and closeness in every touch, not just a quick, Saturday night routine performed without much foreplay and generally in silence.

Now he had gone, I hardly missed him. I was strangely content and found it hard to describe. There were days when I succumbed to loneliness and wandered from room to room scarcely knowing what I was doing or what the time was or where I was. Sometimes I wept and did nothing. Sometimes I just wanted to sleep the time away and not think anymore. Those times were few and mostly I was content. I know people whose unhappiness seems to have no bounds, or is defined solely by what they don't have rather than what they do. My neighbour Diane will always be, in her mind, the betrayed wife. The woman who couldn't keep her husband, who lost out to someone better, someone who satisfied him more, was sexier, prettier, younger, had more to offer. Oddly for me, there seemed to be more purpose to life now that I was on my own. I can come and go as I please, eat when I want and I have lots of friends who I can now spend time with.

I had been planning some new décor for the bedroom, I guess partly to infuse some new life and energy into it, and I planned to do more painting and a flower-arranging course. Sadly my social life was almost nil and I did miss having a man around. Brian could always fix things or know someone who could.

Now my boys are grown and living their lives; Joe, my youngest, backpacking in Australia before going to university in Newcastle, and Nick pursuing his career in film-making in Pennsylvania, working on a huge documentary about the American way of life, so I was free to do whatever I wanted.

I decided to take Tally's advice. I'd almost forgotten what it was like to laugh and play with a man. I'm almost sure that there was a time with Brian that was fun, but it seemed a million miles away. However, I was determined that that was about to change. I would take Tally's advice and get out into the real world and enjoy life to the full. It was just so difficult to know where to start, where to go at forty-plus to meet people and how to go about attracting the right person. 'Must have a good sense of humour, must be loyal and truthful, but most of all must see life as something to be explored, laughed about and enjoyed   rather than endured'.

13

So, I had to start somewhere; I needed to get my hair done, grow it longer perhaps and buy some new clothes. Tally could help me upgrade my wardrobe if funds would allow. She had such good taste and I had become rather predictable and unadventurous, so I could start by buying something colourful and a bit more up to date. I'd always wanted to wear red but Brian had convinced me it was cheap and a bit flashy.

Scarlet, yes, definitely scarlet!

And some new underwear too. Time to be a bit flashy perhaps!

***

CHAPTER 2

Having recently been made redundant from the estate agent's office that I'd worked in for ten years, I'd managed to get a temporary job in the local school just a few minutes walk away from where I lived in Stokesley. I was getting on with life quite well really but had become a bit of a hermit. That had to change.

It was only two days later in the local gardening centre that I met Stuart. I was waiting for an old set of garden shears to be sharpened. One of the advantages of only working part-time was that it gave me the opportunity of getting some necessary jobs and repairs done.

"Hi," said a voice next to me. "Are you buying a lawnmower?"

"Are you selling one?" I'd replied sarcastically as I turned.

"No," his expression changed and he grinned cheekily. "They do sell them here you know. I'm sorry I was being forward."

I didn't respond but I heard him take a breath.

"I saw you and thought you looked so attractive and so nice, and I wanted to speak to you. It was the first thing that came into my head." He was gazing at me with a sheepish grin.

"I'm waiting for shears," I muttered, knowing that I was blushing. He looked away, embarrassed, coughed and then his expression changed.

"Yes, right, I'm Stuart Preston."

He held out his hand, which I ignored but replied. "Hi, I'm Laura Goddard."

"Well, hello," he grinned. "Can I buy you a coffee after you get your shears?"

"Sorry, I'm on my way to see my solicitor and I'm running late."

"Are you getting divorced?" he asked, looking at my wedding ring.

"No, not at the moment. I've decided to stay married." *Why did I say that?*

"The best ones are always married," he smiled. "Can I have your number if you change your mind?"

When did men get to be so cheeky? I thought.

I looked at him properly for the first time during our conversation. He was quite ordinary looking, brown hair and soft, limpid brown eyes like a spaniel. He looked scrubbed and well groomed. His clothes were dull but expensive-looking and he was definitely a bit younger than me. He had 'nice' stamped all over him, and had what I can only describe as a 'sweet expression' and I was tempted to give him my number just because he had made that half-hearted suggestion.

Was that what I was looking for? I'm not sure anymore. I gave him a small, regretful smile. "No, sorry." So much for my intentions of having some fun with the first man who wanted to give me some! How extraordinarily pleasurable it had been to be asked. I was flattered of course. This was the sort of thing that happened to other women, not usually to me.

My shears returned, I smiled a goodbye to Stuart and inwardly thanked him for making me feel good. *OK, the wedding ring must come off,* I thought, that would make me feel more available. Certainly the divorce was almost 'absolute' so I had to get used to not being married. *I just don't know how to flirt,* I thought. Perhaps I should take some hints from my more adventurous girlfriends. *I'll ask Teresa, she's a bit of an expert on dating.*

Her fluffy, blonde hair and lovely white teeth attracted men easily. She manages to talk, laugh and joke with men without any embarrassment and had been internet dating on and off ever since it started in the late eighties having lost her first husband in a car accident. She had a teenage son called Harry from her first marriage.

"Teresa I want to ask you something rather silly," I said later on the phone. "How did you get to be so good at getting dates and having fun?"

"What do you mean?"

"I was chatted up today and I didn't... couldn't... hell, I didn't know what to do or say. He was such a pleasant bloke too."

"Did he ask for your number?"

"Yep, and I said I was married."

"Idiot."

"I still am until the end of this month, but I just felt so unprepared and silly. I would liked to have seen him again," I'd explained, realising how ridiculous I sounded. "I'm forty one and I just don't know how to respond to a man, don't know how to react. I haven't dated at all, ever. He could be an axe murderer or something. How would I know?"

"Darling, you would know. You always suss people out really well," Teresa said airily.

"Yeah, good at sussing out women, but I have no parameters with dudes."

She'd laughed. "Join an internet dating site, Laura, and meet a few people. Everybody is doing it. It will at least give you some practice and even if you don't like 'em you can practice on 'em. I go out with loads of men and I am still practicing just in case I get to meet the 'one'. Update your look a bit too and buy a few sexy clothes."

Teresa always looked sexy. Although she wasn't tall, she had the sort of voluptuous body that looked good in anything. After she lost her husband she got her life back by living it to the full. That was until she met and married a charming Irish rogue who left after only six months for a nineteen-year-old, so she decided that she would stay on her own, for a while at least, but she had a lot of fun and endless dates. Teresa was still really looking for Mr Right and reckoned you had to kiss hundreds of frogs to find your prince. She is searching for love with the hopefulness of a twenty-year-old, but occasionally I found myself envying her chaotic, self-centred life. There have been a couple of frenetic relationships that had, at the time, seemed to have been the 'one', but Teresa's need for emotional excess usually brought about the inevitable loss of interest and a bit of self flagellation, until the world righted itself again and off she went, hell for leather back into the dating scene without a hint of the trauma she had apparently experienced. She was brilliant at closing doors behind her.

"It's time you had some action, hon."

"Isn't that a bit risky?" I asked.

"Not if you're careful," Teresa had replied. "I'll come over and set you up. I'll show you what to avoid too. There are some right 'numpties' out there. Some real con merchants too. I had a mate who sent money to a guy she thought was in the US and going to be the love of her life, and he turned out to be a well-educated Nigerian who was part of a group looking for desperate middle-aged ladies to con out of their money. She was devastated. God, can you believe it? He told her they would get married and live in his pad in the south of France... but he was in some diplomatic service and had a problem that he couldn't get out of without a big lump of money, and she fell for it! You do have to be careful. There are loads of scams going on." Then she added. "And, you need to get some condoms."

Hey ho, now that would be novel. I had been on the pill for years but stopped taking them when Brian had left. Apparently, according to Teresa, it's the STDs that are the worry now and even

HIV had moved into the now more freely, active groups of society: the separated and divorced especially the older ones who did not use contraception at all.

At that moment I was fairly sure I wouldn't be needing them, but I'd get some on my next shopping trip just in case. It all felt a little bit desperate. I was determined not to turn into a boring old lady. I was looking for a bit of life and perhaps the discovery of my sexual self *and* a social life. So with a certain amount of trepidation, I got onto the internet and filled in the necessary information. MakingDatesForYou.com promised to find me the man of my dreams. Now I needed to write a profile. There was plenty of advice online but I felt I needed Teresa's help.

The next day I'd finished work early and Teresa was coming over for supper and to help me with my profile. It was a wet, miserable day. I arrived home to find Flo sitting forlornly on the front door step and a letter from Maria, an old friend who was now living in Tenerife. It was her sixty-third birthday that December and she was having a party.

Maria is a flamboyant redhead who used to live close by and babysat when the boys were small. Her second husband had died, leaving her a comfortable widow so she had taken off and bought a lovely old house in Tenerife, made many new friends, entertained endlessly, had met the rather eccentric Hamish who apparently adored her. She always came to see us when she came back to England. She had heard about Brian leaving and suggested I go and have a break with her and her now 'live in' lover Ham. It was her birthday on the fourteenth of December just after my job finished at school and why didn't I help her celebrate? *What a lovely idea,* I thought. Maria would know all the locals and already be searching out the available men she knew. She was an inveterate matchmaker and I needed all the help I could get if I was going on this website.

I would look for a job in the New Year as Brian had suddenly been exceptionally generous at the end of the summer with his bonus from his company. Obviously feeling guilty after the telephone

19

argument, he had sent me a cheque 'to spend on something 'special', so I felt ready to be a bit self indulgent and decided that if I was careful, I could easily afford it. After all, the boys would not be home soon and Christmas would be a quiet affair.

I'm a..."What am I?" I asked Teresa later while trying to write a suitable profile. "A middle-aged woman who has no idea what she is looking for, but knows she needs to learn to laugh again and HAVE SOME FUN."

"Don't just say that. It will be read as sex and I guess that you are after more than that. You need to make yourself sound interesting."

"But I'm not. I really am not the least bit *interesting.*"

"Yes, you are. Let's see... You do yoga -- you are creative, just look at your beautiful house -- you paint, you love your garden and your cat. You're a great mum and you're kind and considerate to everyone."

"That's not very interesting at all."

"OK, so we spice it up a bit."

I have to admit that the profile Teresa wrote had to be modified after she left. It was out and out untruths, suggesting I had travelled extensively. I've only been to Jersey, Malta and Cyprus. That I had a brilliant job and an executive position on the board of the local education department -- I was in fact an admin clerk dealing with everyday correspondence in the local secondary school -- *and* that I lectured on garden design. I once talked to the women's institute about drying flowers from their gardens. I seriously could not live up to those claims, and it was going to be difficult enough making conversation with strange men without telling out and out porkies. She did however choose my online name: LOLLY, which I liked even if it was a little zany.

20

So I wrote: *'I'm happy, sincere and honest. I'm a spiritual person who believes in taking care of the world we live in, giving out good energy and being non-judgmental and kind to others. I work in education and I am interested in so many things: history, yoga, architecture, wildlife, herbs and plants. I love my friends, beautiful gardens, roses, daffodils, hot chocolate, plums, animals especially cats, modern art and ballet. Looking to meet a genuine gentleman for outings and to share my last Rolo!'*

I'd managed to download a photo taken in the garden the previous year on a fine hot day with a glass of what looked like wine but was just apple juice, and I had on a reasonably pretty dress instead of my usual gardening shorts. Tally had taken the photo and I was laughing at something she had said. Practically all my albums are filled with the boys and groups of friends. Anyway, it was the only good photo I had of myself on my own so, onto the site it went. I thought it looked rather good too.

Click, and I was in. Paid my fee. Now I'd to wait for an approval and the acceptance e-mail and off I go. Another glass of wine to celebrate my step into the unknown. What on earth would my boys say if they knew their mother was on a dating site? I hadn't seen either of them since Brian had left but I had tried to explain to them both so that they wouldn't be too hard on him. I know that he would be devastated to lose his sons.

When I finally managed to get hold of Joe on the phone, he was on a train going to Adelaide. He was very non-committal and was only concerned for me. 'Did I want him to come home?'

"Absolutely not," I'd told him. "I'm really OK Joe. You enjoy your time away. You've worked so hard for it and you will be back soon. Please don't worry." I knew he would of course, he was deeply sensitive and even though he didn't express it, would be very concerned about the breakdown of his family. He adored his Dad.

"Just keep in touch so I know when you'll be back. Love you loads, Joe... and so does your father."

21

"Yeah, right. Love you too Mum, but know I'll come home if you want me to," he said sadly.

Nick's attitude was "Go get some counselling." A very American sentiment I thought. He was after all living in a place where marriage breakup and divorce was a way of life. "Work it out Mum, you can't just give up on him." He thought his father needed his head testing and put it all down to a mid-life crisis. He would speak to him soon and tell him exactly what he thought of him.

"Nick, it's gone past the counselling stage. He's already living with her and I don't want him back."

"Seriously, Mother? After twenty-three years. Are you sure? Hell, I knew you weren't madly in love, but never thought you would split."

"Sure, I'm sure. Now you get back to work," I'd told him.

He promised to get in touch with his dad and he never told me what had been said, but I continued to get long concerned e-mails. He might try to get back for Christmas, he said, but I knew he wouldn't. His work and his life were both satisfying and he was happy, so that was all that mattered. He had recently met a new girl, Paula, who seemed to be taking up much of his spare time. He'd mentioned that her family had asked him to spend Christmas with them, so I was very much resigned to spending Christmas without my boys around. Joe would be back January or February and then straight off to University, but I would see plenty of him as he was going to Newcastle just a few miles away.

***

22

CHAPTER 3

I can only say I was completely staggered by the response to my newly accepted profile. I opened up the site after having my morning coffee and had six messages and eight winks on day one. I looked at those who had winked at me. I didn't think I could respond to a wink. What do you say to someone who has closed one eye for you and you didn't even see it? Munching my buttered toast, I sat at my computer and read and re-read the following:

1. LEMONken. 24. Virgo from York. 5'9"

Lovely lookin' bird get in touch Ken x

2. Jimbo. 42. Gemini from Leyburn. 5'7"

Hello, how are you? You look and sound like my perfect woman. Can we chat? Jim.

3. KMGrant. 45. Libra from Heckleborough. 5'3"

i am keith a fun guy with my own howse and car i have two childs with me on a regula basis so idont get much out i like gardenning, in fact i am emploed part time as a firman and the rest of the time i wok at the local old folks home gardenning.

4. Stantheman. 44. Scorpio from Stainton. 5'10"

Lolly are you fo likkin xxxxxxxxxx

5. WillIDo. 48. Virgo from Knaresborough. 6'0"

Hello beautiful lady. My name is James and I am sure we have a lot in common. I do not like messaging much so if you give me your number we could chat on the phone. If you prefer I will give you mine. Hope to hear from you soon.

6. Happyharry. 44. Aries from Egton. 5'11"

I am looking for a companion to go walking and hiking with, etc, etc, etc!!!. Are you game enough to tackle some serious exercise???

OK, so only number two and five would get a reply and I'd ask them for telephone numbers so that I could call them. Teresa reckons that is the safest way to get in touch and to suss 'em out a bit.

Oh dear! Let me see.

LEMONken. Number one is twenty-four, almost the same age as Nick, no way!

KMGrant. Number three has got to be a dyslexic and an illiterate midget I'm sure.

Stantheman. Number four is looking for a leg-over and reading this message, I was tempted to change my online name.

I'm not sure what Happyharry number six is looking for?

Neither of the profiles of numbers two and five had said much about themselves, and Jimbo number two had no photo as he said he couldn't manage to download one as yet. His profile said he had three children and a dog, a hamster and two rabbits, and he liked fishing.

The photo of number five, James, was a full body showing a slim, tall man in walking gear. His profile was short and to the point. *'Looking for interesting lady to wine and dine, hold hands and enjoy the good things in life.'* I have to start somewhere so let's give them a chance. What do I say? Just be your-self, I thought. So with shaking hands, I typed a reply to Jimbo Jim and Willdo James, both the same: *'Thank you so much for your message. As I am not very good at communicating in this way. Would you like to chat on the phone? If you would like to give me your number. I will happily call you. LOLLY.'* Oh dear that sounds so formal and straight-laced. Should I say something encouraging? Should I be a bit flirty? So I had added, *'I am looking forward to meeting you.'*

Oh really, Laura, I thought. *Is that the best you can do?* I'd be surprised if I got a reply.

Teresa says it's like buying the perfect pair of shoes; you just have to try loads before you get a right fit, style and the perfect colour. She also told me to act and speak as if I was doing an interview so that I didn't go out with someone highly unsuitable even if he did have a good telephone manner. Find out as much as you can about them and always meet in a public place.

Right, I determined. *I'm ready, I'll call them both if they send me their numbers.*

The day was bright and sunny for a change, so I got into the garden to do the inevitable autumnal tidying and forgot all about my messages. The garden looked sad at that time of year and an early frost had killed off all the geraniums and dahlias, so I spent a couple of hours gardening, pottering and planning my trip to see Maria in Tenerife. I'd have to get a move on because her birthday was less than eight weeks away. How lovely though to be going away from the cold for a week.

I had no time to fret about my failed marriage. Although I still had to keep reminding myself of the fact. I had plans and I was '*on the loose*' for the first time in my life as an adult. As I finished in the garden, the sun was going down and the October chill returning but I was quite content and was feeling good about making changes to my life. The prospect of going away, seeing Maria and meeting new people was beginning to excite me. I was free to do whatever I chose and so I decided to make the best of it.

Jimbo had left me his number almost instantly. Now then, how hard could it be to telephone a potential date? I lifted the phone and dialled. He answered almost immediately, catching me off guard as I was still practicing what I was going to say.

"Hello I'm Lolly. Well I'm Laura really," I spluttered and gave a self-conscious laugh. "Is it OK to speak to you?"

"Yes, yes of course. Nice of you to answer my message."

Jim had sounded pleasant enough and asked me all sorts of questions and chatted easily so I didn't feel I needed to talk a lot. I wanted to ask him things too but before I realised it, we had made a date to meet in the car park of a pub about halfway for us both for the following day.

My first date. I was terrified!

Having spent ages getting ready the next morning, I was sitting in my car in the car park of the 'Golden Lion' in Northallerton taking deep breaths and trying to remember everything Teresa had told me, when a little shiny, red face appeared next to my window. He was short, pudgy and had wispy flyaway hair. His excitement showed in his wide grin and protruding eyes. He was dressed in a green corduroy jacket over a yellow shirt and baggy beige trousers.

"'Ello, 'ello, Laura, my lovely," he said and my heart sank as I got out of the car. He was at least three inches shorter than his professed 5'7" and he looked grubby and unkempt.

Ten minutes later sitting in the bar with a cup of coffee, he was showing me pictures of his three children, all of whom looked exactly like him with sticky up hair, huge ears and the same pop-eyed expression. Loads of pictures too.

"This one is at the fair and these at the zoo last week, and here they are at my sister's birthday party."

"They're really lovely," I said, disgusted at my own hypocrisy.

He puffed up and smiled. "I've some pictures of Fluffy, our dog, too." His pudgy little hands fiddled with the phone while I wished fervently that the time would pass and I could escape. He leaned closer to me, and yes, the dog looked just like the children. I caught a whiff of his dreadful breath and leaned back in my seat.

"Lovely," I said, now ashamed of myself for feeling superior and condescending. He was obviously proud of his brood.

Finishing my coffee, I stood and muttered a 'thank you' and said I must rush home as I was expecting a visitor. I really was by that time feeling appallingly bad as he had obviously come with great expectations and kept telling me how attractive I was, asking when would we meet again as he was having such a lovely time and how we had really connected. *'No way, Jose!'* So trying to avoid making any further arrangements, I thanked him profusely for the coffee and strode quickly toward to my car. Looking back to the doorway, he was standing waving with a sad little smile, but fearing he would follow me, I sped off with a quick wave.

So much for internet dating, I thought. I wanted to get home as quickly as possible and couldn't even think of ever doing that again.
However two glasses of wine later, I checked the site and found I had another four messages, and James had sent me his telephone number so I thought I had better make the best of it. I had, after all, paid my fee and reckoned I was unlucky to pick such an unsuitable guy for my first date. I should have listened more carefully to Teresa's instructions. She obviously knew what she was talking about when she said to find out as much as you can. Sipping my third glass of wine and feeling slightly inebriated, I phoned James and found it much easier to talk to him. I asked him loads of questions and found out he didn't have any children: one star, and he was definitely 6' tall: two stars, and he had black hair: three stars, and he thought I looked adorable on my picture: four stars. Not bad. I was obviously slightly tiddled, but managed to scribble in my diary a date for the following Saturday.

At least James was quite good looking and had a fine, well modulated voice that made me feel more at ease than I had with Jim. He was lean and well dressed, and on first take, looked sexy and appealing. However he turned out to be a real whinging bore. We started well enough and settled into a seat by the window in a cosy little bistro that he had suggested.

After chatting for a few minutes, he said, "At least you look like your picture. Some of them don't, you know. I went out with one girl who had put her sister's photo on the site because she was better looking." He laughed but then continued, "I don't really like internet dating because women tell lies… especially about their age and their weight… Really I'm serious," he said, regarding my amused expression. "Another one I went out with described herself as cuddly and she was at least twenty stone. Had a job to roll herself out of her car."

"Don't men tell lies too?"

"Dunno, do they?"

"Apparently mainly about their height and their jobs, or so I have been told," I said brightly. "I haven't been doing this long."

"It hasn't worked for me."

"Why do you continue then?" I asked.

"Don't know really," he said. "I guess I just wanna believe that there is a perfect woman somewhere out there for me."

I wanted to tell him that according to my friend Teresa there were quite a few men on the site who found telling the truth difficult too, but I listened to his dating stories for about half an hour, all of them with deceiving, greedy or baggage-carrying females who had disappointed him. One had managed to have at least three dinners out of him and he was peeved. Was he peeved!

"I think there are so many takers on this site. I can't tell you what it's like for a man to be taken for a ride."

"Oh… really… I don't know. What do you like doing, James?" I asked, trying to change the subject.

"I play golf in my spare time but not much else. I have a really responsible job, you know. I'm an inspection engineer and my speciality is industrial drains. I have to travel quite a lot, go all over. I was in Edinburgh last week and Exeter the week before so I don't have much time for women. I guess I have just been unlucky," he sniffed, "not having met anyone yet. I could do with somebody to come home to. I'm a bit fed up with ready meals."

"Aah... Right, so you are looking for a housekeeper really then?" I said sarcastically.

The expression on his face changed and he tapped his fingers on the edge of the table. I think he'd already made up his mind that I was another that wasn't right for him. So quoting my wise and worldly yoga teacher Eloise, I said. "Well, James, everything in your life is a reflection of the choices you have made."

After paying for my own coffee so as not to be added to his list of greedy females, I hot footed it home and wondered what on earth I was doing looking for a date like this.

Snuggling up that evening with Flo at my side and a glass of Rioja, I decided that internet dating wasn't as much fun as it was made out to be. I would call Teresa and have a bit of a giggle about my 'hot' dates.

"Don't give up, hon," she'd said when I told her about my pudgy little gnome and my whinging willy James. "Remember what I said, my first internet date turned out to be a cross-dresser, who asked me how I'd feel about him wearing my panties... Well, you can guess what I said! The second one wanted sex in the back of his car and reckoned that's what most women were looking for." Teresa said, laughing, "I told him I wouldn't even want to exchange spit with him never mind anything else. Hell's teeth, I have been out with some 'hummers' but every now and again you get a good one. I have had some absolute crackers too. Don't you remember the guy who took me to the premier of that Bond film and then the Keith who took me to Greece for a week? Not that that worked out well as he

29

farted like a buffalo and snored like a hammer drill... but honestly don't give up."

Teresa's latest squeeze was a fifty-something solicitor called Victor and the only problem from Teresa's point of view was that he had two teenage children who spent a good deal of their time staying with Victor and ate, drank, lolled and moaned about his house so it took a week to get rid of the mess they left. Apart from that, he seemed to be keeping her happy and together they achieved a gentle peace that Teresa had not had with other men. The nicest thing about being with them was seeing how much they enjoyed each other's company. They talked and joked non-stop, Vic laughing happily at Teresa's showing off and silly expressions, and Teresa responding to his wit and good nature generously and easily. They had arranged to spend the weekend together in a romantic little hotel in the Lake District for New Year so I had promised to see her before I went away as I knew that she had her 'ne'er do well', son Harry and slightly dotty mother Megan for much of the Christmas holiday.

Several dates later and with a heavy heart, as none of the men I met had been more than a little pleasurable, I came to the conclusion that I'd learnt little about flirting and not had much fun at all. I'd met Kevin, was definitely married, unattractive and even admitted that he was only looking for sex. Then there was Peter with the terrible teeth, never married and so shy I couldn't get him involved in any real conversation at all and gave up when he said that he needed the toilet for the fourth time. Another was called Will, a farmer with a comb over and a huge beer belly who looked older than his professed forty-six years and he smelled like fertiliser. And Jeremy who had a huge black moustache, which he stroked and twiddled constantly as if it were a favourite pet. Two others I could barely remember as they were so dull. Perhaps I was dull too, but I'd tried hard to look good, ask loads of question and I'd smiled until my teeth hurt! I found myself wondering if all the really interesting men were spoken for. I suppose at my age that was probably true as I got plenty of messages from very young guys or widowed or divorced, sixty-year-olds who.

Never mind, I thought. The following week I was ready to go off to Tenerife, my packing all done and arrangements made with a neighbour to look after Flo. Maria had phoned and told me that the weather was good and I was to bring something special to wear for her party. I decided on a long, honey-coloured chiffon dress that I'd bought for an Easter holiday with Brian in Malta two years before, but had never worn because it had been so unexpectedly cold in the evenings. I remember that he too had been unexpectedly cold. I had known, of course I had. While I perhaps didn't understand, I'd turned my back and let myself believe that Brian's secrecy, his evasiveness and cool behaviour was just who he was. I'd put it down to his extra workload at the time but now know only too well the reason for his sulkiness and early nights.

***

CHAPTER 4

I had one more date before I went away and still being the optimist that I am and recalling what Teresa had said, I'd persevered and phoned MrLookingForYou, from York 5'10". His profile was long and interesting and he had recently come back from working in the Far East. His age was stated as forty-eight and his profile picture showed that he was good-looking in a tanned, relaxed sort of way that appealed to me. We messaged and he gave me his number.

After talking to him on the phone, I was really excited. His name was Gordon, and having asked about my family and interests, was keen to meet me. I asked him loads of questions too which he answered with an amused aside to his voice. He was working, he said, on a large-scale investigation into drug smuggling as he was in a special international police force highly trained for such a job. He told me he was divorced and apparently in a position that he was considering retiring and writing a book about his travels and exploits. He sounded so confident and genuine that I promised to meet him the next day. He had a morning commitment in York, where he was staying so I said I would drive there and meet him for lunch, so we exchanged mobile numbers in case either of us got lost or delayed. We settled on a small coffee shop that I knew and I was looking forward to going to York for the first time in ages.

Coiling my hair into a smart French pleat and wearing my shiny black, high-heeled boots, new scarlet fitted jacket over my also new, rather tight and expensive black jeans that Tally had helped me choose, I thought I looked really different to my usual sweater and trousered self. I added a jaunty red, black and white soft woollen scarf and off I set.

Parking outside the city walls, I walked past the Minster and through the Shambles. Admiring the Christmas decorations I thought to myself, *I should come here more often. It is such a lovely place.*

Years ago Brian and I would come to the theatre here and I had a moment of sadness wondering if those years had really been happy or had I deluded myself even then. I can mainly remember his insistence that we should only see plays by well-known, serious playwrights and he never indulged me when I wanted to see musicals or new writers.

It all seemed a long time ago and now I felt optimistic about life and would definitely go and see as many musicals as I could afford. It was a fine, bright day and there were many tourists and Christmas shoppers around and I got a real buzz from the beautiful, bustling atmosphere.

I arrived at the cafe early. All the little tables were taken so I ordered a coffee and contented myself with standing by a shelf, which stretched along the back wall. Over the shelf was a noticeboard advertising everything from crystal healing to a local amateur production of 'Blythe Spirit'.

Amongst the posters, I saw an advert for a company who needed someone to market a new art product and travel around the area selling to art shops. I took a note of the number as I was still looking for an interesting job and although I knew little about art products, I did paint a bit and was really interested in trying new ways to improve. One of the things on my 'list to do' in the New Year was to join a painting group or an art class.

Sipping my coffee, I used the noticeboard as a distraction as our meeting time had passed and I was hoping that he would turn up soon. How awful to be stood up on our first date but I considered waiting for at least half an hour as it had taken me longer than that to drive here. I was just about to phone him when he came bowling in through the door.

He recognised me immediately and kissed me on the cheek. He was apologetic for his lateness and I liked him straight away. He was well-built, a rugby player type with large hands and feet, a

33

lovely head of dark hair with a sprinkling of grey at the sides, and dark hazel eyes. He was charming and good-looking in a rugged sort of way. Conversation was easy and he told me he had been married twice, and had four children and two stepchildren in various parts of the world. He must have started very young because his oldest son was in the States working for the government and his youngest, coming up to eleven, was in France with his mother.

I enjoyed his company and found him amusing and really interesting. He had been everywhere and lived for several years in Australia and Thailand. He had loads of tales to tell and explained about his book and what he intended to do with it, how he apparently wanted to expose loopholes in European law that allowed drugs to be brought easily into airports and ports.

We talked for so long that after lunch, we walked along by the river and stopped in a bar and toasted each other with a glass of Chardonnay. I felt terribly attracted to him and wanted to touch him. He was looking out across the river and as I watched him I thought about him lying naked next to me and in my mind, my hands were caressing him, and stroking him, moving about his body exploring every curve and contour. I felt unbelievably guilty having such thoughts. He turned to look at me, smiling and making some remark about boating in the summer and I found my stomach clenching and knew I'd find it difficult to respond to him or anyone else at the moment. Brian had left me for a woman who had been more attractive, interesting and exciting than me. My ego was much more bruised than I had previously admitted to myself. Brian had told me, quite unnecessarily, when he left that he had never felt for me the attraction that he felt for Sophie and that had really hurt me.

"So what are you looking for, Laura?" Gordon asked, cutting in on my thoughts. I hesitated and wondered if he was reading my mind. Then he said, "In a man I mean. Are you looking for a long-term relationship? Children?"

"Oh God, *no*, I'm far too old for that, I don't really know for sure what I am looking for… I guess some male company. No, I don't mean just company… You see, I don't know really. I just feel well... I've missed out on a relationship with any meaning… *you*

34

know," Oh, hell. I sounded like an imbecile, but I carried on. "I haven't... you know... actually, I'm sure you don't know but I have only ever known one man, so you see I have nothing to compare, and... " I stopped stuttering. "Sorry, so sorry I can't explain. I must be off now. Need to feed the cat."

"Are you looking to get laid?" he asked with an amused expression. He reached toward me and took my hand in his and I noticed again how large his hands were. I blushed from my toes to my hairline and pulled my hand away. I stood feeling like a schoolgirl.

"Laura, there is no sin in being inexperienced. I bet you have always been a good little wife and your husband a wham-bang man. Am I right?" he smiled knowingly. "Meet me after your holiday… yes?" He leaned forward and kissed me on both cheeks, took my arm and walked me back to the car park.

I left feeling foolish and my earlier euphoria was now in my boots, so to speak. I drove home wondering why I couldn't just go along with my feelings. Why did I feel so embarrassed about being touched? Why was it so difficult to respond? After all, I was answerable to no one. I'd felt that ever since discovering Brian's betrayals I'd been shutting off my feelings, biting my tongue to avoid expressing what I really felt. I was no longer sure *what* I really felt. I knew that I wasn't unhappy, but I'd extinguished something of myself; the open, responsive confident self that I used to be. Although I could think and fantasise about sex with someone else, I wasn't sure how to let my body respond. It had sort of shut down, gone to sleep.

Perhaps it was the way I was brought up. Going to an all-girls school hadn't afforded me much insight into interacting with the males of the species. My dad found the changes taking place in the 60s and 70s all a bit confusing as he was a staunch chauvinist who believed women should be cared for, but know their place. I was expected to be articulate but not too clever, capable but passive and positively accepting of male supremacy. As I matured, I realised dad's ideal for a woman was totally out-dated and seemed to be based on my perfect mum who had died when I was only nine. When she died, her image accompanied me all the time, and believed I would never get used to her absence, but now my memory of her was vague. She was passive and gentle and allowed my dad to be in charge and he was always the one I counted on to get me to school, make sure I had everything I needed and laid down the rules about bedtime and such.

I don't know how we bear a loss so great or how we recover, but time passes and although I could still remember her smile and her smell, the impact that she had on my life had all but disappeared. Consequently my father was over-protective and strict, and as I grew up, we weren't really very close so when Brian came along he was the answer to Dad's prayers. Neat, clean cut, ambitious with a good family background. What could be better for his little girl?

Dad was now in his late seventies and living with his sister Margaret in Leeds who had never married and was happy to have him there and although I saw him often enough, we didn't really have much to talk about. He had a comfortable, peaceful life and found it difficult to upset his routine of bowls, bridge and cricket umpiring and even when he came for Christmas, he couldn't wait to get home again, and more so now that the boys were grown up.

When I told him of Brian's affair and subsequent abandonment he was very upset, "I don't have a lot Laura but I can always help you out if you need it." His main concern was whether I could manage financially.

"Thanks dad, but I'm OK, so don't worry. As long as Brian continues to support Joe when he goes to Uni, we'll be fine."

"Don't be on your own. I'll come up and stay awhile if you like. Christmas is coming and the first one alone is always difficult," he'd said knowingly and a little sadly.

"No, Dad. I don't want to upset your routine."

"Well, we do have a rather important match next week."

36

"I know… it's really OK," I'd said.

It must have been hard for him when mum died. He'd never complained and I was very aware of how difficult a young daughter must have been for him. He was a great dad, if a little strict, but his good Christian principles had held me in good stead. I felt a wave of warmth for him as I'd never gone short of love or affection. I went through the usual teenage traumas but ended up doing well at school.

Being with Brian and encouraged by my dad, I'd spent my teenage years in dreams of married bliss, two children and a house in the country. So dreams do come true: but not always as you expect them to!

Best not to expect dad to come for Christmas, I thought.

I knew it would be difficult, and at that moment I had no plans at all and I certainly didn't expect my dad to watch me wallowing in self-pity, which was what I was expecting to be doing. Neither did I think either of the boys would be home.

On the evening of the fifth of December, two days before I set off on holiday, Teresa and I met for a drink. I'd walked to the local pub in the cold, wet weather and arrived looking like a drowned rat. Vic had dropped Teresa off outside and gone off to see his sister. He'd promised to pick her up at ten thirty so we intended to have a drink or six, and put the world to rights.

"You look bloody marvellous," she said, as I arrived at her side, a gin and tonic sat on the table waiting for me.

"I'm soaked," I said, taking off my coat and pushing my fingers through my hair.

"You still look great. I hope Maria has someone good lined up for you."

"So do I… thanks," I said, picking up and slurping my drink, "though I'm sure every man in my age group will either be married

37

or have a big chip on his shoulder, or there will be some other good reason he doesn't have a partner, probably gay or weird. Oh, I don't know. The truth is I met someone I really like just two days ago and I'm going to see him when I get back from Tenerife." I told her about my meeting with Gordon and how pathetic I'd been, how I'd hotfooted it home after his question about whether I wanted to get laid. I didn't expect Teresa to understand as she was so experienced and sure of herself and followed her basic instinct wherever it took her without a seeming care in the world.

"I'm on a promise when I get back from holiday. I'm going to try not to be such a pain," I smiled, "but I'm shit scared."

"Are you ready to get laid?" She lifted a questioning eyebrow.

"Yep, I think I am in my head... In my head I'm definitely ready, but do you know, I just start to panic at the thought of it... I'm getting a bit worried that I won't be able to respond or that the bloke won't fancy me with my clothes off. My body isn't what it used to be, you know. I *have* had two children... and... well, how long can you hold your tummy in, for heaven's sake? Have you ever looked at yourself in the doggie position without clothes?"

"Just don't get on top," she laughed, "and candle light is good if you're so worried. It gives a bit of mystery too, but you know men like a bit of flesh whatever the mags say. Look at me," she said and thrust out her ample breasts and slapped her midriff. "Keep moving, Babe, and they won't notice, but cover up quickly when you've finished. Men have a wonderful ability to concentrate on the good bits. Get yourself a bit tiddled too, alcohol definitely helps you loosen up. Champagne is the answer, really turns me on, I've been known to push my luck a bit after too much champagne. Come on, let's have another G and T, and you can go and get it and flirt with the bartender. I know he's not your type, but just practice. Go on, you'll be in Tenerife this time next week, surrounded by admirers and I want to hear that you had some fun while you were there."

Standing tall and pushing out my chest, I approached the bartender. I could see Teresa making signs at me, egging me on. So feeling I could try, I swayed a bit and then leaned forward across the bar to the podgy, rather bored-looking bloke who was absentmindedly polishing a glass.

"Two G and Ts please," I said in a flirty voice, turning my head to the side, blinking rapidly and twiddling a bit of Christmas tinsel that was adorning the bar round my forefinger. I smiled broadly. To my surprise, he responded instantly, put down the glass and said with a wink and a sly little smile, "Of course, Madam, will that be all? Is there anything else I can do for you?"

"Yes, no. That's all, thank you" I said and returned with the drinks to where Teresa was grinning at my discomfort. So much for flirting. I'd have to practice being a little more subtle. I know I'm always impressed by women who do it naturally, flicking their hair or holding their chin in their hand and getting that sort of round pout that I admired in some of my friends when they were around men. I was aware it didn't come naturally to me, so practice I would at every opportunity otherwise I'd be frustrated forever and never have any fun. Teresa insisted I flirt with every man who looked in our direction, so I tried lowering my head and looking up and smiling, it really wasn't that difficult and halfway through the evening a hairy, rather macho type sent us drinks over. I lifted my glass and smiled my 'thank you.' Teresa was impressed when he approached us and I just said, 'thank you' again and carried on my conversation. Feeling dismissed, he wandered off. I knew I was blushing. I just had to stop being so self-conscious.

We chatted and laughed the evening away and I told her about the job that I'd seen advertised. Although I'd scoured all the papers and the job centres, I hadn't found anything else that appealed to me. I decided that before I went away, I would call the number and find out more.

Another gin and tonic, and I felt the holiday mood increasing and my excitement mounting. *Tenerife here I come,* I thought. When Vic appeared in the doorway, we finished our drinks and left.

"Have a lovely time, Hon. Don't worry about the job until you get back," Teresa advised as we put on our coats. "Just concentrate on having a good time. Come on, it's chucking down. Vic will give you a lift home." Opening her handbag, she produced a tiny wrapped Christmas present.

"Oh Teresa thanks. You'll have to wait until after Christmas for yours, sorry," I said and mentally made a note to get her something in Tenerife. Other than being inundated with Christmas carols and hoards of people indulging in retail excess in the shopping centres, I'd managed to give it little thought. I really am an all-or-nothing person.

In bed that night with Flo curled up at my feet and still feeling a bit tipsy, I thought about how inept I had become through lack of practice in the flirting department. I decided whilst I was away and *if* I got the opportunity, I would try making some smart, witty remarks and use a bit of body language like leaning in, face touching and hair flicking. If the opportunity arose I would take it. I think I'm ready now!

***

CHAPTER 5

The plane was full and the journey uneventful. Sitting next to a pleasant Finnish lady who talked in broken English almost all the way made the time pass quickly. Hamish and Maria were at the airport to meet me and greeted me with warm hugs and kisses.

"Oh, my darling girl, I'm so pleased you could come. This is my Ham, quite a lovely chap he is," Maria said as she patted his shoulder fondly. "We have more than an hour's journey to Puerto de la Cruz so we can catch up. Must say you look lovely. Doesn't she Ham? Are you hungry? Thirsty? Do you want to stop on the way?"

"So pleased to meet you, Laura," Ham interrupted, and with a warm smile, took my suitcase, said firmly, "Lets go. Now stop fussing Maria."

He was a large, soft-bodied man with a mop of rather unruly gingery hair and a full beard. His arms were hairy and his legs, which were protruding from a pair of rather garish red and blue shorts, were also covered with coppery fuzz. He had an interesting lined face of someone who had lived in the sunshine for a long time, and I could see instantly why Maria found him attractive. His voice was deep and warm and he looked directly into my eyes as he spoke. I was already sure that I would like him, certainly far more than I'd liked Ted, Maria's now-dead husband. Ted had always treated Maria's slightly eccentric, arty personality with disdain. He was a staid accountant who dressed permanently in grey, whereas Maria adored bright, sometimes flashy colours which, often clashed with her red hair.

I loved her exuberance and often wondered how she had got together with Ted. Still, he had left her extremely well provided for which enabled her present life style. My boys had adored her too and always wanted her to babysit them when they were small. She invented children's stories or retold old ones, embellishing them along the way.

We chatted non-stop all the way to their home in Puerta de la Cruz and Ham drove his battered old Citroen rather fast but skilfully along the coast road. It was dark when we arrived but the night was warm and the sound of the sea below the cliffs was lovely. Such heaven, to be transported away from the hard, cold wind and rain of North Yorkshire to this delightful island.

Maria's house was perched on a cliff top and had three floors. The lower was embedded into the rock face with an enormous terrace, a pool, a large kitchen and a storeroom in the Spanish style reached from both a staircase in the house and one down the side of the rocky black cliffs from the front garden. Lots of sun beds and umbrellas, great pots of flowering shrubs and purple bougainvillea grew along the sidewall. The first floor housed a lounge / diner with huge windows and a wooden balcony overlooking the rocky seashore, a kitchen, one large bedroom with an en-suite and a study piled to the ceiling with art and books. Yellow and cream walls housed bright and exotic paintings. The floors were covered with multi-coloured rugs. I was taken to the top floor, to a lovely, rustic bedroom with a small balcony on which pots of red and white geraniums sat dancing in the light evening breeze. It had old, Spanish, dark wood furniture and a huge bed which was covered with a white lacy counterpane. A bunch of white daisies sat in a painted jug on a chest of drawers, which gave the whole room the impression of a romantic Victorian attic. It was heavenly.

I was, by now elated and tired and after a light meal. I'd intended to get an early night but the wine and conversation flowed well past midnight and I finally flopped into bed, happy and slightly drunk, at about one a.m.

"Lie in, sweetie and we'll get you up for lunch," Ham had called as I weaved my way up the creaky wooden staircase.

"Okay dokay," I'd said, but after a lovely sleep I was wide-awake at seven thirty a.m., the sun was shining onto the sea and the birds were singing. I lay, watching the breeze swishing around the plants on the little balcony and was aware that I felt so good and relaxed. I am so lucky to have such amazing friends. This past year they have loved and supported me through all my resentment, consternation and sadness of being abandoned by Brian. I no longer cried or felt sorry for myself as I had in the beginning, and I know that Tally, Teresa and now Maria were part of my healing process.

My lovely yoga teacher Eloise too had been surprisingly supportive and given me some simple affirmations to get me through the worst times and I'd used them at first not understanding how powerful they were. "Good words and thoughts create a good life," she'd said. "Create your own reality with positive words about yourself and your circumstances."

I'd said every morning since, 'Today is a beautiful and special day and I am surrounded by hope and love' and every night. 'All my needs are satisfied', without really believing the possibility of the improvement they were creating. This morning, I knew they worked. Here I was in a beautiful place, with beautiful people.

Over the next few days, Maria and Hamish took me into town to some of their favourite places. We went to a little village in the foothills of the volcano El Teide which was covered with snow and pretty as a picture, visited a theatre in Los Realejos to see a local amateur dramatic group, drank Sangria in the sunshine in La Pas in a street cafe under yellow umbrellas, surrounded by purple bougainvillea and cream hibiscus flowers. We enjoyed the restaurants and cafe bars, ate local fish with sautéed potatoes and spicy spinach, met friends, sang along to a Spanish guitar in another bar and watched the sea rushing against the rocky shore in Puerto.

What a thoroughly lovely week!

I shopped for colourful kaftans: pink and soft grey for Teresa, and emerald and cream for Tally, and bought the boys baseball caps with 'Puerto' embroidered on them. They always had a huge selection and wore them everywhere. At least they *did*. It had been eleven months since I've seen Joe and fourteen since I'd seen Nick.

Ham took us everywhere, pointing out beautiful scenery and historic architecture. He was an artist who had a divine sense of humour, totally irreverent and slightly over political, who had lived in various parts of the continent for the past twenty-five years. He never mentioned having a wife or family, and I didn't ask. He was obviously madly in love with Maria who treated him like an adored pet and laughed at his silly jokes, teasing him about his pot-belly and laughingly likening his hairiness to an orang-utan.

They were delightful company. Maria was happier than I'd ever known her. Her red hair was now helped along, but was still long and lustrous, clipped up untidily. Her waist was slightly larger and her walk a little slower, but she looked magnificent in her kaftan-type blouses and long skirts of peacock and gold. Her jewellery also reflected her larger-than life character, long knotted pearls, chains and beads in rainbow colours that swung as she walked or she held them against her ample bosom.

During the week, we shopped for candles, wine, champagne, beer, cocktails and huge bunches of flowers for her party. A caterer was bringing all the food, which was to be typical Spanish tapas style and would be served on the vast terrace over-looking the sea. Potted palms and flowering plants decorated the area, and narrow steps led down to another small terrace cut into the rock face with seats and blossoming shrubs there too. Tiny rows of solar lights led the way and ran along the walls just enough to see the steps. To the left, the town of Puerto de la Cruz twinkled, and the sea crashed on the rocky shore below. The rock on this part of the island is volcanic and black as the night itself. The weather was good, if slightly breezy, but typical for that time of year.

In the afternoon of Maria's birthday, I helped Ham and his friend Samuel drag chairs and tables from the storeroom, and arrange candles and flowers everywhere. From rising that morning, Maria had been smiling. I had bought her a little clock encrusted with Whitby jet which she loved, as she was born and bred in Whitby. Ham had painted her a picture, which he had been secretly working on at Samuel's house for the past few months. Maria squealed with delight. It was remarkable and not at all the style I would have expected Ham to paint in. It showed the back of a couple entwined, looking into a misty distance. They were surrounded by soft, smoky surreal birds and mists of butterflies. It was without doubt the most romantic picture I'd ever seen. It had a look of Gustav Klimt but with softer edges and colours. Maria was entranced, and kept kissing him affectionately on the cheek so that his smile widened and he was putty in her hands, especially when she explained the layout of the tables, chairs and flowers that he was expected to organise, apparently not a task that he was inclined to be enthusiastic about. He saw his role in the proceedings as a distributer of alcohol and mixer of cocktails. Nevertheless he carried out the tasks willingly and appeared at eight pm ready for the party, dressed in a superb pair of turquoise-blue trousers with a cream shirt and matching bow tie. Maria looked stunning in a long, loose purple and turquoise creation that wafted in the evening breeze, her red hair pinned up with a matching pin. What a colourful couple they looked.

The guests trickled in over the next hour or so all bearing gifts for Maria. They were introduced to me as they arrived. First to come was Jorje and Sylvi Gomez who spoke little English but were charming. Then came Amy and Pierre, brother and sister, French I thought, who were visiting the island. Both were startlingly handsome and well dressed. Amy chatted for a while about how lovely the island was at this time of year and how her writing always improved after a visit. She explained that she was a freelance journalist working mostly in France and sometimes the UK. She had amazing blue eyes and was wearing a dress that complimented them perfectly, and her glossy brown hair was cut in a fashionable bob. Her brother was tall and fair but with the same colour eyes, and they were indeed the most good-looking pair there. Amy wandered off to chat to Samuel and the rather squat lady called Ampara he had brought to the party with him. She was good-looking and typically Spanish, with a mass of dark hair and a wide glossy smile. She laughed loudly and obviously knew everyone as she greeted all who came, with double kisses and big hugs.

I was introduced to Hilda and Gregor Bachmann from Germany. She was a long thin streak in a grey silk dress, which trailed the floor, hair a blonde pompom and her mouth a fuchsia slash. She surveyed the scene with half-closed eyes like a contented lioness. He, on the other hand, was rotund and balding, had twinkling eyes and a mischievous grin and an unlit cigar clamped between his teeth.

So many people of all ages and nationalities: Mandy and Grant from Liverpool, a young couple running a pool cleaning service on the island, Elise and Joseph from Russia, a couple from Belgium, and another from Holland, many locals and several of the English and Germans, mainly retired, who lived on the island during the winter months. Some people came on their own, including a handsome Spaniard called Juan, another called Gervais from France, two elderly, English brothers Andrew and Michael, with their sons Roland and Christian who were only in their twenties or early thirties.

Gervais led me away to dance with him as soon as he had downed a couple of drinks and old Andrew winked at me as I was swept around. I was having such a good time and Maria looked pleased when I told her so. The music was loud, and Ham and Maria danced and sang to everything, Ham puffing and sweating, encouraging his guests to get up and dance. Everyone drifted to and from the pool area where the food and drinks were being served.

I danced with Juan as Tom Jones sang 'Sex Bomb' and then Grant from Liverpool asked me. He made me laugh with his enthusiastic jumping and wriggling.

During 'Dancing Queen', Ham swung me around until I was breathless and had to have a rest, so I wandered over to the bar for yet another glass of champagne. I stood watching with amusement the stiff legged, strutting antics of Lotte and Vincent and the exuberant wriggling of Mandy, whose bright red dress encased large, bouncing breasts that jiggled around like a pile of golden blancmange. Both Roland and Christian watched her with wide-eyed amazement and admiration. Grant was giving a good impression of Elvis Presley, and Ham and Maria were still circulating around their guests, obviously having a great time themselves.

***

CHAPTER 6

Out of the corner of my eye, I became aware of a movement from the staircase from the upper garden. The gate swung open from the outside steps and a beautifully dressed, powerfully built man in his forties stepped through. He was dark haired and had a thin tanned face with an obviously broken nose. He stared through everyone with a blank expression until his eyes alighted on Amy and his face lit up. Seeing him, she turned her back on him and continued the conversation she was having with her brother and Samuel. He started to walk towards her but before he reached her, Maria was at his side, taking his elbow and leading him towards the table set up as a bar. His eyes didn't leave Amy until he was handed a large glass of wine and Maria was bending her head towards his and speaking earnestly. He smiled then and showed a row of white teeth. The two of them headed toward the terrace wall and were deep in conversation when Ham said behind me, "Funny old situation with those two, Luis and Amy." He'd obviously watched me observing the scene. "They clearly love each other but Luis is so jealous he has almost driven Amy away, won't give her an inch and is always accusing her of cheating on him. He is a good bit older than she is and she is such a looker, is she not? Maria only invited him to the party if he promised not to cause any trouble." He raised an eyebrow. "Don't want any trouble on Maria's birthday now, do we?"

In the meantime Maria had led Luis toward another couple and was introducing them to him. Amy had disappeared into the kitchen.

"He is very attractive," I said to Ham.

"Yes, isn't he? Money too, old Spanish family. They have houses here and in mainland Spain but he was educated in the UK. Married some dotty English girl who left him for a toffy-nosed lecturer at Cambridge. Don't know the details, but it was a bit of a relief for the family as she didn't like them and never visited. Luis has a big thing for Amy though. Met her here you know… two years now, but they rub each other up, you know how some people do? Know they love each other to bits but can't seem to make it work."

Luis had turned around and was facing us so Ham stepped forward, and gestured toward me.

"Laura this is Luis Perez de Falla… Luis come and meet Laura Goddard, an old friend of Maria's from North Yorkshire, in England." Luis's smile made his whole face look different and he took my outstretched hand in a courteous old-fashioned way, slightly bowing his head.

"I have heard Maria talk fondly of you. Very pleased to see you here, Laura."

We talked for an hour, Luis replenishing my drink and bringing me tempting morsels from the table. He was amusing and interesting, and I found myself flirting with him. I cocked my head to the side as I spoke and then felt rather ridiculous because I thought I must look like Tally's spaniel waiting for a treat. I held his gaze a little too long and pouted my mouth just a little. I must have been doing very well because he said, "Come, let's dance."

He led me to the small area on the terrace where everyone was gyrating to George Michael. Hilda and Gregor were standing close together rotating their hips around in time to the music. Gregor still had the unlit cigar between his teeth, a comfort thing he had told me as he was trying to give them up. Mandy and Grant were singing loudly and out of tune, but they were having such fun. Luis held me close and I found myself happily leaning into his tall muscular frame. We swayed to the music and I could feel a lovely, tingling warmth enveloping my body.

Mmm, this is delicious, I thought. My face must have reflected my pleasure.

"What are you doing that is so different? You have a serenity that is beautiful."

I laughed. "If only you knew."

"Knew what?" he asked.

He took my hand and we moved away from the dance floor and leaned against the terrace wall. It was cool and dark now with stars twinkling above us. He turned to me and said. "Tell me, Laura."

"Things that have happened to me in the last year. A real journey… an eye opener. I am like a fluttering bird on the inside and… so unsure about everything really. There are so many things that I have learnt about myself and my life in the past few months. Never realised my life was so 'not normal'."

"What is normal? You mean your marriage? Maria told me that you are on your own after more than twenty years. So strange for you, no? You'll find another. You are beautiful. You shine, Laura."

"Shine?"

"You do."

"My husband didn't think so."

"He stopped looking at you. Marriage is so unromantic. Now the courting *is* romantic. Marriage has to be willed to be successful, love does not make it so, that is too easy. Love drives but does not 'glue' people together in marriage."

"I can't get my head around that, Luis. Surely love is the foundation."

"You'll see," he said knowingly, "people must 'glue' not just love. Love has to be there of course, but it is the 'glue', which forms the commitment. Love comes and goes like the breeze."

"And you, Luis. Do you love or 'glue' with someone?"

"Ah, you mean Amy? I love Amy but I do not 'glue' with her. No. We have no future together."

"But you want to?"

"Everyday I want to," he sighed, "but I know in my heart that she doesn't want me. She is young and ambitious and will leave soon. No, we have no future together."

For a moment he looked sad and then angry but, as he glanced around he said, "You see, she has gone already. She does not care for me."

"Ham thinks she does."

"No, she'll leave for Paris soon and I'll go to England on business in the spring so there is no future for us."

I thought again how doors are closed on relationships, sometimes in the moment of recognition that they are over. For some, it is over time, but men seem to be able to do it more easily than women. I could be wrong but I felt that at that moment, Luis had made up his mind. In a long moment, Brian had decided to leave me. Once he had made that decision, he never looked backward over his shoulder to check where my feelings were. For me, closing the door on our twenty-plus years of marriage was still so difficult and I often wondered if it were all a dream. The only reality of our lives together lay with our two boys.

Luis leaned toward me and for a moment I thought he would kiss me but he reached to the bush behind me and plucked a single apricot hibiscus flower. With a flourish, tucked it behind my ear. "There, it matches your dress. So pretty." I felt like a schoolgirl as my heart fluttered and my pulse raced. I realised that I wanted him to kiss me; there was an electricity between us and we moved toward each other as if in slow motion. He looked into my eyes and raised an enquiring eyebrow. Taking my hand, he led me down the narrow stairway to the lower terrace, which was dark and secluded from the upper levels.

Right Laura, I thought, *this will be good practice.* I felt my tired, dried-up body responding, telling myself that this was exactly what I needed to do. My confidence growing by the minute, I leaned forward, put my hand on the back of his neck and drew him towards me. The kiss was delicious and I could taste the wine on his lips as I allowed my tongue to gently trail his mouth. I'd no other thought than the pleasure of this handsome man. He smelled divine and I'd had enough champagne to feel myself moving into the moment without a qualm. As our bodies moved together, his hands dropped to my buttocks and he lifted the skirt of my dress so that they were pressed onto my tiny panties. He slipped his thumbs into the top of them and pulled them down in a second. The caress of his fingertips set me quivering, one finger exploring the inner curve of my behind whilst the other cupped and squeezed.

The sound of the party above had all but disappeared and I realised how late it was. Would we be missed? Perhaps not. Amy had left, as had a few others before Luis and I came down the dark steps together. We would certainly hear if anyone else came, so throwing caution to the wind, I undid his trousers and lifted out his throbbing penis. All I could think was, *I've never held another man's penis.* It was hot, long and smooth and felt quite different to Brian's short, rather fat, circumcised one. With it released and in my hand, Luis moaned and said something in Spanish. I moved with the rhythm of his body and to my surprise found myself responding. My body, held in check for so long, was burning with desire. Luis lifted my dress up around my waist and pushed my panties down further so that I could open my legs. His words were in Spanish and I've no idea what he was saying but it sounded endearing and romantic, and I'd decided that I'd go with the moment and enjoy it even if it meant getting fucked on the garden wall amongst the exotic foliage.

Moving slightly to the left to avoid the prickly bougainvillea, I leaned backwards and perched my bottom on the wall. Luis fingers were now exploring me and my body opened to meet him, even though I was acutely aware of the hanging plants trailing down the wall under my bum. To my surprise, he released me momentarily and pulled a packet from his pocket. My God, I hadn't thought of protection. Previously, I'd been on the pill for years so had only used a Durex on a couple of occasions after the birth of my sons. Skilfully he rolled it on and slid into me, and before I had another thought, I was moving with him. He clasped my bottom and lifted me towards him so that he could penetrate me more deeply. I wrapped my legs around his body and thrilled with the sensation of being filled. Luis grasped my hips, kissed me hard and passionately while his body moved faster and faster. I quivered with the delicious feeling of him buried deep inside me. Luis was kissing my neck and I was shuddering with delight. At that moment, I felt we had both moved on.

Suddenly, from the terrace above, we heard a noise, loud and shrill. The music had stopped too. Immediately Luis moved out of me and carefully lowered me so that I could put my feet down. We were both still hot and trembling. Now I could hear Maria's voice screaming Samuel's name and the sound of rushing footsteps. Without a word, Luis zipped up his trousers, smoothed his hair, took a deep breath and leapt up the stone steps toward the noise. I looked at myself standing with my panties around my ankles, my honey chiffon dress all crumpled and at my shaking knees. I was still throbbing with desire, but the moment had gone, so thinking only of what was going on upstairs, I quickly pulled myself together, picked up the abandoned condom which I tucked discretely into my knickers, took a deep breath and pushed my wobbly legs up the stairway.

Ham's body was lying by the pool and Maria was holding his head against her breast. She was sobbing his name over and over, her red hair fallen and dishevelled. Ham's eyes were closed and his mouth open. Samuel was holding Maria's shoulder and speaking Spanish into the telephone. Andrew, a retired doctor, was on his knees beside Ham and holding his wrist. As I stood at the top of the steps, I heard him say that it was a heart attack and Samuel spoke rapidly into the phone. The remaining guests were milling around looking shaken and worried. Hilda was holding her hands over her face and Gregor had his arms around her, his cigar still unlit.

"Oh Hamish, you *foolish* man," Maria kept repeating while stroking his forehead. He had been rather overdoing the dancing and his body was drenched in sweat. His eyelids fluttered and by the time the medics came, he was conscious and his breathing had improved.

Very soon, Hamish was being lifted onto a stretcher and away to the local hospital. Maria went with him and as I was staying in the house, I took it upon myself to see everyone away with promises of phone calls about Ham's health as soon as I knew anything. Samuel arranged for Ampara to get a lift home even though she wanted to remain and help, but he and Luis stayed and together we gathered the music equipment, the glasses and ashtrays and tidied the terrace. The caterers took most of the dishes and helped stack the chairs, and as a sharp wind was rising, we moved most of the things back into the storeroom and the kitchen. Luis remained stern and we said little to each other as we cleared the party remains until eventually we were on our own in the kitchen and he turned to me and said, "I am *so* sorry, Laura. I couldn't... "

"Look, I know, couldn't be helped... You don't think I expected you to... *well,* carry on in the circumstances," I said, remembering the condom tucked into my knickers.

"That was no good for you or me. I will make it up to you, I promise. Let us wait to hear about Hamish, eh?"

Samuel came into the kitchen carrying the last of the glasses, which we stacked into the dishwasher.

"Come on you two. I think a stiff brandy is in order," he said and led the way upstairs to the lounge where we sat waiting for news, and sipped Ham's best brandy.

Samuel paced the floor until Luis told him to sit and we waited, passing the time talking about how bad it could be and of friends and relatives who had had heart attacks and were still OK. Silly chat really, and we were all so relieved when at about three am Maria phoned to say that Hamish was doing fine and being kept in for observation but the heart attack had been small with no serious

54

damage done. The doctor had told him to refrain from dancing and drinking for a while. She laughed rather loudly when she said this and we knew it was just the relief because a second later, she burst into tears. "I thought I had lost him, Laura," she sobbed.

"I know, but he will be fine. It's just a warning, I'm sure."

"I do hope so. I'll stay here, I think, and come back with him tomorrow. What a perfectly lovely day it had been until then... Silly man dancing like an eighteen-year-old. I can't tell you how many times I had told him to take it easy. Thank heavens for Andrew. I'll see you all tomorrow."

Somehow we said our goodnights, and Samuel and Luis departed, promising to return the next day, leaving me in the now-rather-sad, empty house. I very carefully wrapped the condom in several layers of paper and took it to the outside bin with the thought that I was definitely going back on the pill on my return home. Then I locked up and made my way to bed. I did wonder why Luis hadn't opted to stay with me. Perhaps he hadn't quite closed the door on Amy after all.

Without my lovely hosts in the house, it seemed gloomy and depressing but I was tired and so relieved that Ham and Maria would be home the next day.

Before I knew it, I had slept and the sun was rising to another lovely bright morning. I found some bread and eggs, made myself breakfast and then spent the morning sitting on the terrace reading in the bright sunshine. There was a light breeze and the sky so sparkling blue I thought again how lucky I was to be there. Luis arrived at eleven thirty and told me Samuel had gone to the hospital to ensure that Maria and Hamish got back home safely. He held my arms and looked into my eyes saying, "What a holiday for you, Laura."

"I know, but it has been wonderful. So lovely to be here in the sun when everyone at home is freezing. I don't want to go back."

55

"It has been good this week. Sometimes we have very much rain here in December, but I think we have had our share this year; we had floods in March, you know."

"Really?" *Why are we talking about the weather?* I thought. He looked disarmingly handsome this morning and I was tempted to put my arms around him. A little shiver swept through my body when I thought of the previous evening, and I could feel myself responding to him again. I wished that I'd met him earlier in the week or even earlier that evening!

"When do you go home?" he asked.

"Early on Tuesday. Only two days left now."

"Ah, I have business tomorrow but I'll take you to the airport on Tuesday as Hamish won't be allowed to drive for a while. It looks as though we aren't destined to get together. I would so liked to have got to know you better. Perhaps I could call you when I am in England? Although you are in North Yorkshire and I don't think I will get there. So sad, lovely Laura."

Never mind Luis, you have done my confidence a power of good, I thought. *I really am beginning to feel positive about myself and if you do get to call me, I could always get on a train to London or wherever you are*, but I said, "Please call me anyway."

"I will," he replied, but I wouldn't hold my breath. This was the sort of man that could attract women anytime, anywhere and our lives were a million miles apart.

Maria and Ham came home about one pm and although Ham was looking well, Maria wouldn't let him do anything, and she and Samuel settled him on the terrace with a blanket and a book. The weather had turned slightly cooler and there was a soft breeze. Luis said his goodbyes and promised to pick me up on Tuesday morning to get my lunchtime flight back to Newcastle. He kissed me lightly saying, " It will be a pleasure, Laura," which made Maria smile and wink at me.

"No," I said quietly to Maria, and went out to sit with Hamish and Samuel whilst Maria went to organise some lunch.

"Made a bit of an arse out of myself, didn't I?" Ham smiled. "I've had to promise to take it easy and behave my age… no dancing… no booze… *as if.*"

"You must do as you are told, Ham. It would break Maria's heart if anything happened to you. I hope you have a lot more happy years together. I want to --"

"I'll keep my eye on him Laura. He is my best mate and I don't intend to let anything happen to the old goat," Samuel interrupted.

Maria arrived with a tray of tossed salad, cold meats and humus, fresh bread, a bottle of wine, and orange juice for Ham.

"Oh, cripes," he muttered as she handed him the glass with a determined smile. He did however drink it and promised to stick to a good diet and no alcohol until he was completely better.

The next day, my last, Maria and I took a little walk to La Pas, stopped for coffee and sat in the morning sun. She looked tired with the worry about Ham, but she was so relieved to have him back. "He's so good to me you know, Laura. I've never had such a relationship before. It is difficult to describe when two people have that special thing… It's like we have known each other through many lifetimes."

"Perhaps you have."

"Yes, perhaps… I hope you find someone to share your life with. Don't leave it too long. Time passes so fast as you get older. I feel that I mustn't waste a single day. Find yourself a good man, Laura." She took my hand.

"I thought I had one."

"But he didn't make you   happy."

"No, but I didn't know that until he left. Isn't that the strangest thing? I had never really thought about it like that before.

***

CHAPTER 7

I was away ten days and leaving my dear friends Maria and Hamish was difficult. They'd given me such a lovely holiday. I said goodbye to Luis at the airport with exchanges of phone numbers, but I knew that I wouldn't see him again. A very pleasant interlude and such a confidence boost, I would always be grateful to him.

Getting back home, I found loads of Christmas cards and among them an invitation from Gordon, 'MrLookingforYou', to a Christmas party with some of his close friends in York. Just four days before Christmas and his friends Jan and Dave were giving a dinner party for him, partly to welcome him back to UK and partly to wish him well with his new life. He was planning to move to Carlton after the holidays, which would be closer to Stokesley. He'd seen a small house by the river that he thought would be a perfect place to write his book. He told me he would still be traveling quite a bit as he still had some contracted work to finish.

"I should come and pick you up really," he said when I called to accept the invitation.

"Absolutely not," I told him. "The round trip is much too far and it's your party. You can't drive me back if you've been drinking."

"Perhaps you could stay over, although probably not, the house is rather small here. I'll ask Jan and let you know. I'll meet you anyway, as they live down a rather obscure farm track and I want to hear all about your holiday."

Perhaps not everything, I thought.

It was late evening blurring into dusk and really cold and wet. I arranged to meet Gordon at the corner of the road that led into a small village just outside York. My car heater was playing up and the journey had been cold and depressing. The rain lashed against the windscreen as I drove along the country roads and the butterflies in my stomach marched in tune with the wipers.

Talk about 'back to reality'!

I hunched into my woolly scarf and hoped that he'd be on time. I'd decided not to stay over as I really didn't know Gordon and his friends well enough. I wasn't at all sure what to expect.

He'd arrived within minutes, breathless, wrapped and hooded against the cold and rain. He jumped into the car and hugged me as if we were old friends. Seeing him again was amazing. I felt rested and positive from my holiday and far less nervous. I looked good with my glowing tan and had found a way of putting my hair up so that it looked younger and more feminine. I felt much more confident since my intimate moments with Luis.

"So pleased you came," he said smiling. "Good holiday? You look fantastic. Come here." He squeezed my arm, leaned forward and kissed me on my cold cheek, and I was happy that I'd accepted the invitation even though it had meant me driving to York in such awful weather.

A twisting roadway led to a small brick cottage tucked away behind some trees. Gordon showed me where to park and helped me out of the car, and we squelched our way towards the front entrance. Jan and Dave opened the door together and were warm and welcoming. Jan, a plump blonde with spiky hair, dressed all in red with a huge baggy sweater and extremely high heeled shoes had a shiny, round face that had obviously had a bit of lifting with plumped up 'trouty' lips. She never stopped talking, whereas Dave, who was skinny, with long shoulder-length hair and a raggedy moustache, said nothing at all. He had an odd array of clothing, topped with a green and blue striped shirt and a paisley waistcoat.

Not at all what I expected. I wonder how Gordon became friends with such an unlikely pair. From first glance I wouldn't have thought they had anything in common at all, but of course I hardly know Gordon yet. I thought.

Dave disappeared into the kitchen from where there was a distinct smell of burning. Jan kissed me and then took my arm and guided me into their rather disorganised but interesting lounge full of dusty old furniture, musical instruments and books. A wobbly Christmas tree stood in the corner with an assortment of fairy lights and a few presents beneath it. Two large marmalade cats lay asleep among the gifts.

"Milly and Henry are here already," Jan said, indicating the couple who sat on the fat, green squashy sofa, arms wrapped around each other and gazing into each other's eyes. "But we are still waiting for Ray and Ed."

Dave appeared and handed me a large glass of red wine.

"Darlings, say hello to Laura. This is Gordon's friend. Milly, Henry, stop smooching for a mo," Jan said, turning to me and lifting her painted eyebrows. "They have just decided to make a baby. Excuse the mess, darling." She waved her fingers towards the rest of the room. The pair on the sofa turned and said a brief hello and feeling slightly embarrassed, I sat opposite them, moving a pile of magazines to one side. They took little notice of me and thankfully, Ed and Ray arrived carrying armfuls of flowers, Christmas gifts and bottles of wine and tequila and they greeted everyone including me with hugs and kisses. I thought Ed was probably about the same age as Gordon and it turns out, they went to school together somewhere in Lincoln. Ed was thin and camp with mascaraed eyes and glossed lips. Ray was young, probably twenty-five or six, with a youthful grin and a smooth, pretty face.

"What's for dinner Jan darling?" Ed asked. "I'm starved. Haven't had a mo' to eat today. Been fitting curtains all day haven't we, sweets?" He turned and addressed Ray.

Ray nodded and smiled. "Big order though, will get us through the next couple of weeks."

"It will, it will, won't it just," Ed said, clapping his long manicured fingertips together.

"Interior design," Gordon informed me quietly as the men pranced around, opening and pouring the wine before claiming their places at the dinner table. Jan and Dave disappeared into the kitchen, returning a minute later with an enormous lasagne and a huge bowl of salad. Plopping it in the middle of the table, Jan said, "Garlic bread on the way."

"No servers darling?" shouted Ed as Jan wafted back towards the kitchen. "Do you two mind? Come and sit at the table and stop canoodling." Ed addressed Milly and Henry, who were still absorbed with each other on the sofa. They finally seated themselves together, apologising to Ed as he laughingly took the micky out of them. Jan appeared with the garlic bread, waving the serving spoons with another bottle tucked under her arm. In between drinking rather large quantities of red wine, she dominated the conversation talking about friends who had recently got divorced with terrible financial consequences, the state of the roads, the appalling weather, and the cost of Christmas.

Ed and Gordon seemed to have an odd relationship. They obviously knew each other well and whilst ploughing through the first course, recalled several silly episodes from school and stories about their early days in the boy scouts, then laughed hysterically when Gordon related an incident involving cans of baked beans when they had been camping with the scouts. I didn't quite understand what they were laughing about but Ed turned to me and said, "Darling, it was hilarious, you should have seen our scout master's face when he found the tins full of pee and all the baked beans gone. Farting all night we were...trump, trump, trump." He rattled his infectious laugh again. Hard to imagine Ed as a scout but he was obviously a source of amusement even then. I learned that Ed and Ray ran a rather large and expensive shop in Middlesbrough selling designer curtains and soft furnishings. They had been together for about six years and were very successful.

I did try to have a conversation with Henry and Milly but they seemed to be in a world of their own, and contributed little to the conversation, but I found out that they rented a house in York and had apparently previously decided to stay childless because of the sad state of the world, but having recently been working and living in Australia (where they had originally met Gordon), had made a decision to emigrate and raise a family there.

"More stable than anywhere else we have ever been," confided Milly. "We'll get decent jobs there too. We are both teachers, you know. Crying out for good teachers, they are… and well, honestly, the education system here has gone to the dogs, absolute crap now. Bloody interfering policies... can't do a decent job anymore."

They were both in their thirties so would have no problem getting visas, they said. Having worked in a very good school, I wanted to disagree but common sense told me that these two felt very strongly about their profession and how much it had changed for the worse in their years of teaching so I smiled and kept my council. I'd never done any actual teaching but knew that those in my school did an excellent job and seemed to be managing the new policies well.

I noticed Dave said little and Jan drank so much that by the end of the first course she was decidedly tipsy and was slumped in her chair with a piece of Christmas tinsel around her neck. I still couldn't imagine how Gordon had met or become friends with them. They seemed so different to him, but he had been staying with them for two months since his return from Thailand so they must have been close.

"Get the pavlova and the fruit salad Davey, my love," Jan instructed.

"In the fridge, is it?" Dave said, getting up instantly.

"Of course."

It was obvious who was boss in this house and although they were all very friendly, I did feel like an outsider. Gordon was clearly aware of it, as he kept looking at me and winking as if to say he understood. They were a very odd group of people and the

63

conversation was trivial and often about their mutual friends who I obviously didn't know. The whole evening, including the menu, felt a bit like going back in time and reminded me of the early days of my marriage when we asked friends around but had little money spare for entertaining. The lasagne was overcooked and the pavlova soggy, but I seemed to be the only person who minded. I ate lots of salad and fruit, and picked at the garlic bread. The conversation was light and pleasant enough and I found myself warming to Gordon as he drank little, squeezed my leg under the table and listened to Ed babbling on about his business and their plans for a Caribbean cruise in the spring. I watched them all getting inebriated whilst I sipped my tonic water. My large glass of red wine still sat on the mantelpiece. I wasn't going to take any chances driving home at this time of year.

Henry, Ed and Gordon disappeared for about fifteen minutes after the dessert and came back laughing.

"Want some, Ray?" Gordon asked, thumb pointing backwards and a silly grin on his face.

"No, thanks. Not tonight. I've got to get us home."

So what did I think? In truth I thought they had been off for a snort of brandy. It wasn't until several weeks later that I became aware of the truth. God, I was so naive!

When I felt I could, I got up to leave with the excuse of the weather and the journey. Henry and Milly were back on the green sofa, Jan was sprawled over the arms of a chair with her knobbly feet waving about as she'd kicked off her high heels, her blonde spikes resting against a fat pillow, and she was mumbling and yawning. Gordon got my coat and an umbrella and I said my goodbyes, thanking them for their hospitality and wishing them a Happy Christmas. Milly and Henry waved a couple of fingers towards me, Ed and Ray hugged me goodnight and Jan said, "Hey... Yes, Happy Christmas, eh Laura. Lovely to have seen you... met you... yeah." There was no sign of Dave.

It was still pouring with rain and Gordon and I rushed together to the car.

"Thanks for coming, Laura. See you after the holidays when I get moved. Have a lovely Christmas," Gordon said, kissed me, and then ran back to the house.

All in all, a rather strange evening. Not really the sort of friends I expected Gordon to have or indeed the sort of dinner party I'd expected. Perhaps I'd read the signals wrong. I went home with an odd, unexplainable feeling.

***

CHAPTER 8

After my lovely holiday in Tenerife, I had no problem spending Christmas on my own and felt that I'd returned to a comfortable space in my head. Plenty of TV, and a phone call from Dad who was happily eating his Christmas dinner at the bowls club. Joe called. He'd been invited to a beach barbecue, then Nick who was at Paula's parents house in the Hampton's (wherever that was). Teresa was stuck between 'on the edge of dementia' Megan and 'nearly twenty going on twelve' Harry. Tally was with her family in Jersey, and later I spoke to Maria who assured me that Ham was doing well and had curbed both his drinking and his dancing.

I missed Joe and Nick, and the usual Christmas gathering, but surprisingly I was happy that they were enjoying life, and I was quite content with Flo on my lap and a huge box of chocolates supplied by Tally. I had several glasses of Tia Maria with my half a duck 'a l'orange' courtesy of M&S, watched two old films and sang along to 'White Christmas', then fell asleep on the sofa. Not a bad way to spend Christmas Day.

The sun was shining on Boxing Day and I had been invited to my neighbour Diane's house for drinks and nibbles. She kindly looked after Flo when I'd been away so I took her a prettily wrapped selection of toiletries. She had her parents staying and her sister Sue was coming with her two teenager daughters. It was a pleasant, noisy day with the girls. Diane was still not very happy and had made it clear that she didn't like being on her own, was bored and miserable since her husband John had walked out on her six months before Brian had left. I don't think she'd changed anything in her life or come to terms with it at all. She just made a point of talking about the sadistic, nasty man she'd married, given up everything for, believed in and trusted who had so cruelly abandoned her for a 'tart'.

Diane was a few years younger than me. She had told me that she'd never wanted children but whether John was of the same mind I never knew. She had two smelly little Pekinese dogs, which she spoilt incessantly.

"Years younger than him too, and with two brats already," she had sneered. She exuded a nervous, bitter energy and even her own parents pursed their lips when she'd insisted on talking about him. I'd asked if she'd consider joining a dating site and she said. "Oh, no that is just *so* desperate."

"No, it's not Diane. I do it. You need to get out more. It has helped me no end. At least now I have a social life and it's a good way to meet people."

"Men, you mean… No, I'm not interested in meeting *men,* and where is there to go on your own? *Everything* is geared for couples."

"You are still young… why not? You don't have to marry them and there are other things you could do."

She frowned and said again, " No, I am *not* interested."

I'm definitely interested in having a life even if it is without a husband. I am not going to moan, I've decided I'm going to live my life to the full.

The next day I thought I'd better get searching for a job but looking at my CV, I realised it wasn't exactly impressive so I spent a bit of time trying to make it sound more interesting.

Digging out the phone number of the art company, I decided to give them a call and see what they were looking for, only to find a recorded message saying that they were away until the New Year and if there were any applicants for the job could they please phone on the second of January as interviews would be held on the sixth.

Now, must get through the New Year without bawling my eyes out at being on my own.

Teresa was with Vic, Tally still in Jersey and Gordon had already arranged to see relatives in Lincoln and would move into his new pad on his return.

I drank three large gin and tonics, a whole bottle of Cava and didn't see New Year at all until the next morning when I woke feeling sick and miserable. Served me right!

I stayed wrapped in my dressing gown all New Year's Day and refused any calls. I wasn't being unsociable, just wanted to rethink my future a little. So saying my affirmations and planning what I was going to do in the next year, I spent the day deciding what I thought I really wanted. New beginnings,' they say. I say, "OK, I'll give it a go."

I even wrote a list:

New job.

SEX

More exercise.

SEX

Less alcohol.

SEX

See more of friends.

SEX

Decorate bedroom.

SEX

Clean lounge carpet.

Oh well, I could achieve *some* of them!

On January the second I called 'ArtLovers Magazine' and asked about the advertised job. A rather snooty Miss Colleen Glendale-Grey explained that it was a new way to help artists of all levels. The job entailed convincing art shops and outlets that if they would encourage and sign up customers to subscribe to this very new, smart magazine, they would get free advertising themselves. The magazine would promote workshops and courses and use art professionals to advise and extend knowledge of painting and craft. Contributors could send in examples of their work, enter competitions, and attend seminars and meetings in their own area.

"That sounds extremely interesting," I enthused.

"Have you had any experience in selling?" asked the haughty Miss G-G.

"Not much, but I'm very willing to learn. I do paint a little myself." Summoning up a little courage, I asked, "Can I ask why the magazine doesn't just advertise to get contributors?"

"Advertising is getting *so* expensive. We are finding that by using sales persons as a direct link, it makes sure that the magazine reaches the right audience and *of course* the idea to offer free advertising to art shops who signed their customers to subscribe to the magazine helps everyone. We already have reps working very successfully in the South west, Scotland and the Midlands." Miss Glendale-Grey was *very* convincing.

It seemed to me like a really good idea and I was sure that I could sell this. Miss G-G then explained that it did mean quite a bit of travelling and some out of hours work because the proprietors of art shops were often unavailable during working hours. It also meant that to cover the early morning and evening appointments I would be expected to stay away. All leads would be supplied by the company but my appointments would have to be arranged with the proprietors themselves.

Other than my little cat, I had no problem with that, as the company would pay for accommodation and if I could persuade Diane to pop in and feed Flo for me, I'd be more than willing. The salary was very small but the commission was good and the stay-overs would be included. With a bit of persuasion, I got an interview with Miss Colleen Glendale-Grey, the personnel officer of ArtLovers Magazine in Leeds on the sixth January at two-thirty *precisely*.

The office of ArtLovers Magazine was in a fashionable and busy area of Leeds and I had a long walk from the car park so arrived out of breath at two thirty three, just as a beautifully tailored redhead was leaving. Her lips were pursed, her face rather red and she had undoubtedly just been for an interview too, and by the look on her face had already been turned down. She made a derogatory remark about snotty women as she passed by me. Miss Glendale-Grey was waiting and looking at her watch. Feeling terribly nervous, I stuttered an apology. She neither smiled nor frowned and her face was unmoving throughout the interview. Botox, I wondered. I guess she was fiftyish, thin as a broom handle, very elegant, with a huge roman nose and emerald green eyes. I found myself mesmerised by her absolute lack of expression and stuttered my way through the following hour. Not having had the time to summon up the calm authority that I was convinced I could bring to the magazine, and, after an appallingly bad interview and a totally unconvincing presentation about how sure that I was the right person for the job, Miss G-G pushed a form towards me and asked me to fill it in and sign on the dotted line. I couldn't believe it. Her perfectly made up face gave me no indication of whether she was pleased or not.

I had to ask why she'd employed me. She looked at me, pressed her perfectly manicured fingertips together and replied confidently, "You look and sound exactly right and I have a good eye, usually know who can and who can't. Never been wrong yet." She got up from her seat and with a flicker of a smile said, "Get back here on the twenty fourth for two days' training and then you'll start officially the following week."

I got the job… I was *ecstatic*… Woweee! I smiled inwardly as I returned to the car. I was so pleased with myself I decided to go and visit dad and tell him my good news.

He was delighted to see me and very positive about my new appointment, seeing how much it meant to me.

"Suit you down to the ground, my girl. Always said you should do something concerned with art. I can see you are really excited about it," he smiled. It was lovely to see him so perfectly cheerful and happy.

" How are you doing, dad?" I asked.

"Having a bit of bother with my blood pressure, but otherwise I'm well, and still playing indoor bowls while it's so cold outside, and bridge of course."

Reassured, I went home full of anticipation and I couldn't wait to tell Tally and Teresa my news, so, not having seen them since before Christmas, I called them the next morning and invited them both for lunch to celebrate with me and give them their kaftans, and of course catch up on all the goss from Christmas and New Year.

I'd already spoken to both of them on the phone and told them all about the lovely Luis and the party in York. I knew about the fabulous time Teresa had had in the Lake District with Vic over the New Year but Tally had said little about her holiday in Jersey.

"Did you have a good time, Tal?" Teresa asked.

"I did, but Mother and Father did the usual attempts at matchmaking and I met every eligible man on the island from twenty-year-olds to sixty-year-olds but… I did actually meet someone I *really* liked… He's everything I could possibly want in a man; tall, good looking, ambitious, no baggage. But… he was attached of course, wouldn't you know? Has a long- term fiancée and is getting married in May or June sometime. He's gorgeous and I think he liked me too, but he lives permanently in Jersey, for Pete's sake. Just my bloody luck."

"When are you going back?" asked Teresa

"Easter, I hope, and I'll see him I know, but there is no hope for me. God, we got on so well," Tally sighed. "Never mind, I'm still having a great time with Mark."

Lunch with my two dear friends was fun, and we decided to try to see more of each other in the coming year. Teresa's job as a manager for a car hire firm was becoming harder and harder as she was now in charge of all company hire vehicles and her hours were long. Her relationship with Vic was on going though and she seemed happy enough. "He'll have to offload those kids if we're ever going to get together."

"You can't ask him to do that, Teresa," laughed Tally.

"No, you're right… wouldn't of course. But in the end it'll be them or me." Pulling a face she added, "My dear mother is deteriorating fast so I'll have to get her sorted before I can think of myself anyway and Harry is away on another hair-brained idea. He has volunteered to go to some god-forsaken country in Africa on a voluntary scheme that entails counting mosquitos or something. He will of course expect me to help fund him. Jeez I don't know what it's like to have a life of my own anymore." She sighed dramatically. Teresa had always been a busy person and wouldn't have it any other way. She handled difficult situations marvellously well and was never home, dividing her time between her job, Vic and her mum, Megan, her Aunt Grace, plus a plethora of friends and relations.

I was so excited about my new job and told them what it entailed, and we had a good laugh about Miss Frosty Knickers G-G. Then we made plans to get together some time in February, to have a night out or perhaps go to a spa day or somewhere for a real treat, if our jobs would allow. Tally often received complementary coupons from the various hotels she worked for so, she would try to get us some.

I breathed a sigh of relief when Joe came home from Australia on the tenth of January looking fit and grown up. He was taller and sturdier, his hair was longer and blonder and his freckles had increased. As he was getting older, he looked very much like his dad with his fair colouring and pale skin, whereas Nick was dark like me. The year away had obviously done him good and it was hard to believe that he had been gone for so long. He brought me all sorts of little presents; a tea towel from Sydney, a koala from Adelaide, a tiny opal pendant from the Coober Pedy opal mines, and an aborigine painting from Toowoomba. What wonderful experiences he'd enjoyed. I was so happy to see him and for me to be free before the job started so that we could spend some time together while he was home.

We always had a really good relationship and sat into the night chatting and reliving some of his adventures. He'd worked for a few months restoring old cars with a Scot named McKendrick who'd been in Australia for years. He'd taught my son a great deal and Joe reckoned he was going back to Oz when he got his degree. God, how I hoped he'd change his mind before then. I couldn't do with both my sons being thousands of miles away from home.

On arrival at Heathrow, Brian had picked him up and taken him to meet Sophie in Surrey, but Joe was reluctant to talk about his dad, only saying that he seemed happy and Sophie was all right. His body language was reluctant and uncomfortable, and I felt compelled to say something. "Please don't worry if you like her, Joe. I'm really happy for your dad. I realise now that we didn't have much in common anyway."

"It's not right, you being on your own, Mum. What will you do?

I shrugged and gave him a long hug. I knew whatever I said he would still worry about me. I would just have to be OK and let him know that I was. "I manage fairly well, Joe, but there are always things that need doing. I miss having someone around to sort out the practical things... but otherwise, I am doing fine." I laughed.

73

"Perhaps you could cast your 'expert' eye over my car heater while you're here."

"Sure Mum, just give me the nod with anything I can do and I'll try to help."

"Stay around awhile… I've missed you." He gave me a quick hug and assured me that he would.

We spent a week shopping and prepared him to go off to Newcastle, luckily not too far away so I would see him often. We really talked too and spent a lot of time laughing when I told him about my early efforts at dating, and by the end of the week I felt he understood a bit more about my new attitude. I wasn't ready to tell him about Gordon but he knew I was getting phone calls from a man and he wrinkled his nose occasionally when I laughed into the phone or walked into another room to talk.

I didn't see Gordon the week that Joe was home and he wasn't interested in talking about Joe at all, only wanted to know when he was leaving. I noticed a bit of sulkiness in his attitude when I turned down an invitation because I wanted to spend as much time as I could with Joe. Gordon was moving stuff down to his new cottage and told me that his move was nearly complete and he'd be in Carlton the following week.

"Fine," I said. "See you then."

Joe fixed my car heater and moved some garden rubbish for me, and I felt happy and relaxed about having him back home. His course in Newcastle would give him the freedom to come back to Stokesley pretty often, and I knew he would. He joked that he'd come as often as he could, as he would need some good home cooking and a boost or two to his limited finances.

On a cold frosty day I drove Joe to Newcastle with all his gear and tearfully wished him well. I knew he was ready to settle back into the routine of study and exams whereas before his year away, he couldn't face the idea at all.

I met Gordon in Stokesley the following day for lunch as he was still moving his stuff from the various places that he had stored it. He was pleased to see me, and said he couldn't wait to show me his cottage and with a smile added, "Are you pleased we're going to be so close now? We'll be able to see each other more regularly and really get to know one another."

"Of course, I'm sure it will be lovely." I didn't yet know him well enough to be overly enthusiastic.

I wanted to tell him about my new job and my two days' training that were coming up in Leeds. I was excited about getting started but Gordon was too busy telling me about *his* plans and *his* future trips away to take much notice.

I was aware that he was a bit self-opinionated but he was good company and enthusiastic about seeing me on a regular basis, and I *was* having erotic dreams about him… well I *was* having erotic dreams about Robert de Niro and Johnny Depp too.

***

75

CHAPTER 9

It was Saturday afternoon and I'd got back from Leeds earlier than I expected and Gordon had insisted that I go over to his place.

I'd enjoyed my training days so much, met some dynamic people and learned to appreciate Miss G-G as a competent and clever manager. I felt motivated and enthusiastic and ready to start the following Monday. So stopping for an hour at home to see and feed Flo, I quickly showered and changed.

This would be my first visit to Gordon's tiny cottage in Carlton and when I arrived, he had a couple of bottles of champagne in his newly installed fridge. Other than the bedroom, little had been unpacked and the tiny lounge was full of boxes with foreign labels, odd artefacts and battered, well-travelled suitcases. It was lovely, and having looked around, admired the view, we opened the champagne and sat on the bed, toasting his new life. I was keen to tell him about my training for ArtLovers magazine but he had other things on his mind and I felt confident enough to follow him.

"Come here," he said with a twinkle in his eye. He stretched out a hand and drew me into his lap, stroking my back and pulling off the band holding my hair. I put my arms around his neck. I felt the electricity of his desire and was thrilled by it. We kissed, his mouth partly open and I felt it quiver as he waited for my response. I wanted to be kissed so much… I needed to feel desired and although I had some reservations about Gordon, I put them aside and let myself respond. His lips moved to the side of my neck, nibbling and sucking, his breath felt hot and fierce. I liked the feeling and began to relax. I'd had enough champagne to let go of my inhibitions and after my experience with Luis, I felt I could abandon my nervousness a little more than before. I turned, so that he could kiss the back of my neck. I bent my head forward and held my hair to the side as he unzipped my dress and slowly kissed my upper back. His tongue sent waves of sensation down my spine. I felt a little giddy, but my mouth was curling into a smile. Teresa was right, the champagne really had helped. His hands moved to my breasts and were kneading and stroking them making my whole body tingle. Tiny delicious, fluttering sensations leapt around my body and I wanted to laugh out loud at the gorgeous feelings of sexuality stirring between my legs. As he laid me on the bed, I felt a surge of wetness in my panties and I could see his erection pushing against the zip of his trousers. He was quiet and gentle as he slowly removed my clothes.

"Are you OK, Laura? I am happy to go slowly if it makes you feel better."

"Feeling good," I mumbled.

"I'm quite experienced so I *will* pleasure you, you *will* enjoy me. Let me touch you and you will see."

Oh my, I thought, *that sounds a bit... confident, I guess. I had never heard of a man to say such things. He's very sure of himself.*

His eyes were half closed and his head lifted away from me as if he was thinking deeply but he was skilled and experienced, and he excited me physically.

He started to rub my upper thigh and moved his hands and fingers expertly to between my legs. Yes, he obviously knew what he was doing. I felt a little dizzy and knew the alcohol was having an effect, but I was really happy to let go and relax. I'd stopped worrying about my responses or my slightly flabby body.

I reached out and caressed his back, drawing him toward me. He still wasn't looking at me although he pressed his lips to mine. His kisses were sexy and demanding, but without much emotion or warmth. He took my hand and guided it to his penis and moved so that the pressure and rhythm was as he wanted before he let go.

Sex with Gordon turned into a pleasant mutual masturbation session with local climax, but left me wanting. I did in fact have the first orgasm I had had in a long time, but I wanted to ask him what was going on in his head. Even when he entered me, he seemed so far away, not exactly cold but distant and dissociated. I felt I could have been anybody and that his emotional self was elsewhere. He wasn't really selfish, just not very involved, whereas I wanted to look into his eyes, connect and please him. He rubbed himself into me and it felt mechanical. My pleasure was diminished because he didn't look at me or speak to me. He told me to shush when I attempted a few endearments. He said it disturbed his concentration. His huge hands held onto me and moved about my body expertly but he didn't really caress or fondle me as I wanted. Was he following some good instructions from inside his head that he had learnt by heart? I felt a natural desire to stroke and squeeze him and fondle him, but he moved away from me quickly when he'd finished although he did ask, "Did you enjoy that?" He didn't wait for an answer, but smiled as if he knew how much. He disappeared off to the bathroom and I lay quietly wondering if my expectations had been too high. I felt satiated but unsatisfied.

Next time, I thought, *it will be better.* It's just the first time but I was disappointed and now the alcohol felt sour in my throat.

I needed some water to clear my head. I got up, pulled on his shirt, which was lying on the floor and went to the kitchen, found a cup, filled it and drank deeply. The window looked out onto a tiny garden with a hedge on one side and a small field on the other. The view was lovely, the hills in the distance covered with a misty frost, a kestrel hovered over the hedgerow and I could hear the flow of the river. It was certainly the perfect place to write a book. Gordon came up behind me, I turned to him expecting him to put his arms around me but he looked out of the window, his arms at his side.

"Lovely here, isn't it? I'm so glad to be back in England. I'd forgotten how beautiful it is." He was looking off into the distant hills and again, I felt his lack of connection with me. He suggested we go out for a bite to eat as he hadn't had a chance to get much in. His eyes were unusually bright and I couldn't help thinking that he was acting strangely. He had a glazed expression that reminded me how Maria looked when she came round from her anaesthetic after her gall bladder operation. I felt a tremor of misgiving.

"Have you taken   something?"

"What?"

"Taken something, your eyes look odd."

"Pain killers *actually*. I've got a sore back from an old injury, a rather nasty fall in Oz."

"Oh, right."

"Nothing to worry about. OK, let's go out and get something to eat."

Carlton boasted a couple of good pubs, and I was hungry so putting on a smile I said, " Give me five minutes and I'll be ready." The rest of the evening, Gordon was chatty and happy. He talked non-stop about the writing that he'd already started, and said he was excited about the changes he was making in his life. He told me that he wanted to settle down as he had spent so much time on the move and he was happy that he'd met me.

"Lovely afternoon, Laura. Are you free this weekend?" he preened.

"Of course. Let's go and see the new film on at the Odeon," I replied, putting my apprehension aside. I'd had a busy week and was tired, but Gordon's happy mood affected me and I found myself laughing and looking forward to spending more time with him. As I'd had so much to drink, I stayed at the cottage but there was no repeat of the 'lovemaking' that night or the following day, and he didn't get any of the early morning urges that Brian often had. He snuggled up to me and it felt so lovely to feel a warm body in bed next to me, but no, no erection! Perhaps I was wrong but I thought that was to be expected, something to do with hormones and blood flow.

He made me coffee for breakfast but had little else in his meagre bag of shopping, so I returned home and spent the day catching up with laundry and hoovering, and making a fuss of Flo.

After that Gordon and I saw each other fairly regularly and except for my reservations about our sex life and his occasional 'odd' moods, our time together was good. I can't even say the sex was bad. It was just not satisfying. Oh yes, he knew how to excite me physically and I was experiencing some amazing orgasms, but although he varied his 'techniques', they still felt contrived.

We always found loads to do; several visits to Croft race-track, a ride on the Whitby railway train, and we visited endless garden centres where we bought shrubs and plants for his garden and house.

Ray and Ed visited, and treated us to dinner at 'The Tontine'. They were good company, and Ed made me laugh with his stories about himself and Gordon. Ray had masses of common sense and I did think that he was probably the driving force behind their successful business. He listened intently as I told him about my job and the scheme we were selling, while the other two were joking and laughing together.

My social life had certainly improved, although it did vary a bit as Gordon still disappeared for a few days at a time, sometimes 'on business' and once to see his son in France. I had to stay away sometimes too as some of my appointments were early morning or after shop hours which meant I had some daytimes free. There were times when Gordon was quiet and moody and his eyes would wander around as if he was waiting for somebody. He would fiddle with his drink or food or the condiments on the table as if I wasn't there. Sometimes I felt uncomfortable at his sullen glances but quite suddenly his mood would change again and he would smile and start up a conversation as if there was nothing wrong at all.

We stayed together in Gordon's cottage, which was low-ceilinged, warm and had lovely country walks just outside the door. I didn't see much evidence of the writing he was supposed to be doing, and he was happy to go out whenever I was available. He seemed disinclined to come to my house and one of his excuses was that he didn't like cats.

'How can I trust a man who doesn't like cats?' I asked myself, but nevertheless it was early days in our relationship. He treated me well most of the time and although we were quite politically opposed and often had differing opinions about books and art, we got on well. I became used to his grumpiness in the mornings and his occasional moody behaviour.

As time went on, our sex life was much the same and I began to feel that he was emotionally immature and only focussed on a climax, believing somehow that that was all that was needed to satisfy me and presumably those before me. I began to discover that climax isn't necessarily an orgasm. Perhaps it is the other way round that orgasm isn't necessarily a climax. I wanted to believe that a really good true orgasm / climax involved the whole self, not just the physical self.

My fondness for Gordon was increasing and so I tried to express my feelings to him on several occasions when we hit the bedroom, but he seemed to believe because he brought me to orgasm that he was satisfying me. How could I make him understand how much more I needed from our relationship? Soon I became dissatisfied and yes, definitely bored with our 'love making'. I'm sure techniques are fine to know and apply when the mood dictates but they are not the most necessary requirement for a good sex life. Shouldn't sex come naturally to people in a loving relationship?

"Could you look at me," I suggested.

"I'm looking at you."

"No, you're not… you're elsewhere. Are you with me, Gordon or with someone else? Or somewhere else in your head?"

"I'm with you. Now hush and let me concentrate."

"No, I don't want to hush, I want to tell you what I am feeling. You can't pretend that you are 'making love' to me."

"What do you want me to do? Don't I satisfy you?"

"I want you to come close to me."

"How much closer could we get?"

"Emotionally. I don't feel connected to you."

"Oh, don't be neurotic. Just enjoy me. I know you do. Don't complicate things."

Now I was getting angry and rolled away from him. I wanted to tell him how he made me feel, but instead I snapped. "You fuck like a dog, Gordon. Sorry."

"No, I don't. I always take my time and try to satisfy you before myself," he sulked.

"That's not what I am saying. If only you could connect with me on a slightly deeper level… you seem so detached and far away when we make love. Blend yourself into me… Oh hell, I don't know how to explain. Love me a little. I know both our responses would be so much better." I wasn't sure what I was trying to say.

"Oh, for fuck's sake, what are you on about? Why can't you just be satisfied?" he shouted as he left the bed.

"Don't shout at me. I am trying to tell you how-- "

Turning at the bathroom door, he interrupted angrily, "You analyse things too much." Then he slammed the door behind him. I lay gazing at the uneven ceiling and thought of Brian. Why was I thinking about Brian? Perhaps I was expecting too much. I would apologise to Gordon when he calmed down but a few minutes later he came back into the bedroom with a glazed look and a broad smile. He came over to the bed and hugged me tightly. "I will improve darling… I am a bit… out of practice tha's all… tha's all." As he stood he was swaying and smiling.

On reflection, I realise I should have known something wasn't right. Gordon's eyes and smile were often over bright and sometimes his sentences unfinished and incoherent. His mood changes coincided with his addiction to his painkillers, and I became very aware how dependent he was on them.

"How's the job going, Laura? You were going to tell me… haven't said much. You away next week?" He stood with his arms folded, and naked he looked somewhat ridiculous. I smiled and he waggled his flabby todger. He was grinning, but the next minute he was gazing at his feet. "I've got big feet, haven't I?"

"What have you taken, Gordon?"

"Jus' a bit of Charlie." He looked at me then waiting for a reaction.

"What's that? Is it legal?"

Stepping towards me and lifting me from the bed, he said, "You're *so* naive Laura, but you don't need to know. It just helps my pain. Now tell me about your job." He had this silly lopsided grin, and I noticed how dilated his pupils were.

"No… I pulled away. "I want to know… what is it?"

"It's all right… it's my medication, it's prescribed."

"I don't believe you."

"It's not going to kill me," he said and sounded like a childish schoolboy. "And even if it did… what difference… eh… what possible difference?"

"Please don't say such a thing."

"Believe me," he said, "it wouldn't make a difference. There are times when death… dying… is… must be a blessing."

"How can you say that?"

"Because it's true. Life's too damned difficult for some people." He walked to the window and gazed out.

"Some people, meaning you?"

"Yep... Can't be bothered with it most of the time."

"Bothered with what?" I felt myself being demanding and the loving mood slipping away. I was afraid of his answer.

"All the emotional stuff," he said with a sigh, still staring out the window. "I just don't deal with it very well."

All at once, the manic cheerfulness, the moods, the sudden disconnection all started to make sense. Even Gordon's moments of overwhelming affection seemed like dry induced delirium. Watching him, I was aware of how quickly his mood had altered. Minutes before he was warm and loving but then his expression became grim and he had closed up, retreated back.

"How can you say that when you are strong and healthy and perfectly capable of experiencing life to the full. So many can't because they are disabled or sick? How can you be so negative when you are so lucky, one of the haves of the world not the have-nots?" I was beginning to feel angry again and decided to leave. "Anyway you shouldn't be using drugs... I thought you were a fighter *for* the law... especially regarding drugs. Wasn't that what you were *supposed* to be doing? Some sort of specialist... I thought *you* were against drug taking. I thought *you* were on the right side of the law?" I shouted.

His attention had wandered again and he was gazing out of the window. "Yeah that's me," he muttered as I marched through the door.

By the middle of April, my relationship with Gordon had finished when I knew that he was snorting cocaine. I had no intention of continuing to see him. In a way, I was afraid for him. He had been a pleasant interlude and socially, we had had a good time, but sexually

84

he was little different to Brian even if he was more experienced and exciting in the bedroom but not at all emotionally. I just couldn't handle his moods any longer. I wanted more.

Big hands, big feet, big disappointment!

***

CHAPTER 10

Soon after, Tally and I had lunch together in a local bistro. The weather was terrible for the time of year; the trees and plants, heads bowed, weighted down with water looking as if they are just waiting for spring to appear. We treated ourselves to our favourite foods; lobster with a seafood sauce and spicy prawns, and afterwards old-fashioned apple fritters and cream. Nevertheless, we were a pair of miseries together.

She had finally tired of the beautiful Mark, but was missing the sex and seemed very depressed with life. I was beginning to miss the pleasuring I had been receiving from Gordon, and the social life too of course. He had called several times asking me to see him. I *was* tempted but no, I was definitely not having any drugged up, moody men in my life.

Tally looked downhearted and miserable, and as we sipped our coffee, I reminded her of our conversation the previous year.

"Yes, I know, but I think I was deluding myself into believing that it was OK. Well… it's not… I need to settle down."

"You've changed your tune," I said. "I thought it was all fun and games from now on."

I could see from her expression that she was serious so I reached out and squeezed her hand. Tears sprang to her eyes and overflowed down her immaculately made up face. Small rivulets of mascara trickled down her cheeks. She reached into her bag for a tissue and wiped her face, trying to force a smile.

"Oh, Tally, I'm so sorry. What's up?"

"It's my biological clock ticking away, I guess," she sniffed and dabbed the tissue across her cheeks again. "My brother Phil's wife has just had another baby and I want one." The tears flowed freely again and I knew this was serious. The beautiful Tally never cried.

"You want a baby?"

"I want the whole deal; happy family stuff, husband, baby, little house on a hill," she sniffed.

"Little house?" I laughed at the thought of Tally in a little house with a baby and a pair of Marigolds just wasn't on my radar.

"All right then, big house." She smiled through her tears.

"You're serious, aren't you?"

"Mmm."

By now her make up was ruined and she scuttled off to the ladies to repair the damage, coming back minutes later looking as good as new.

"Tally, you've been through all the men in North Yorkshire. How about making a change? Darling, I don't know a single man that is good enough for you. Perhaps you should look elsewhere. Join the dating site I'm on. You'll find loads of... Well, possibly," I hesitated. "It does take time and I'm still experimenting."

"At my age, they're all married or there's a bloody good reason why they aren't. I'm thirty-three soon, you know." She sighed again.

"I know that because I'm forty-three soon."

"Laura, you've done it. Your babies are all grown up and I haven't even started. By the way what has happened to Gordon?"

I didn't want to tell her about his addictions, so I said, "Well, at the end of the day, we just decided that we're really not very compatible... He's too moody anyway."

"Men only have three moods," pointed out Tally, "grumpy, hungry or sexy."

"Ha! You're right. Certainly applies to Gordon… Anyway, I'm glad it's over really, it was far too full on for me and it was getting me down."

"Whatever do you mean? I thought that's what you wanted. Wasn't it fun?"

"Fun? Some I guess… But no, I don't think it was really. I don't know what I want anymore, Tal. I think I'll stay on my own."

"No, you won't. Not for long anyway."

"What about Mr Gorgeous in Jersey?"

"His name is Michael… Michael Parker. I am going for Easter next week so I hope to see him but he will be knee deep in wedding plans," she sighed.

Lunch over we set off into the cold and wet and left with hugs and promises of calls and support for each other when necessary.

Easter weekend arrived and the weather picked up a bit, so I spent some time in the garden, pruning the roses and sowing a few antirrhinums. I missed going out socially but I needed to get over Gordon and his complications, and felt disinclined to see anyone else at that moment. I needed a break from dating so I had all but ignored any messages on the dating site and as time went on, I hardly checked them.

I was so busy at work too and found that I had a good product and could sell the idea easily to art shops as they could quickly see how signing up their customers was encouraging and beneficial. I was moving further and further afield, and could see that ultimately my success would cause me to become redundant. I was sure that was a long way off as Miss G-G had explained plans to extend to art groups and exhibitions to promote the magazine. I had already covered quite a large distance and stayed overnight in

Whitley Bay to see a shop owner first thing and travelled on to an eleven a.m. call in Blyth. Having just the two calls that day, both successful, I had a leisurely drive to Newcastle to spend a couple of hours with Joe. Another day I had travelled to Whitby, then on to Filey and my last call was at seven-thirty in Bridlington so I'd stayed overnight in a lovely little hotel in Driffield, as I had an early appointment in Beverley. My local calls were easy and I wasn't expected to do more than three or four a day. Every day was different and I enjoyed meeting people and earning such good money.

On yet another dismal day, the sky loaded with grey and black clouds of unspent rain, I was in Darlington and had just sold the scheme to a lovely gentleman whose art shop was busy and thriving, but he knew a good thing when he saw it. He reckoned he could easily persuade six customers to subscribe which would give him a new advert. If he could do that every month he would get free advertising all year.

He was showing me out through the door and, without warning I tripped, and fell and only remembered the sensation of falling, then nothing... Couldn't remember a thing after that until I'd heard someone calling my name. Slowly, I'd tried to force my eyes open and turn toward the voice. It was coming through a tunnel... somewhere far, far away, but I couldn't see anything. I was aware of a warm sticky sensation on my face and of being lifted up.

"How are you feeling, pet? Are you OK?"

I'd disappeared once again into oblivion and when I opened my eyes again I saw a pair of soft, limpid brown eyes gazing into mine, surrounded by a mist.

Someone was holding my hand and I had a neck brace on. I blinked several times but the mist kept coming and going. I felt panic rising in me but a soft, calming voice said. "Lay still, Laura." *How did he know my name?*

"You've had a nasty fall. You're in an ambulance going to Middlesbrough General." The eyes looked somehow familiar and I couldn't quite focus on the rest of the face. The voice too reminded me of something… somewhere else.

Some time later I had my eyes open but still couldn't quite focus when the same voice said, "Just going into the hospital now, Laura... don't worry." I think he was still holding my hand and I could hear the swishing of the trolley wheels as we whizzed through the corridors. My mouth was dry and I couldn't make any words and I drifted off again into a dark misty place.

When I finally came to, I was feeling rather foolish as everything returned to normal. A plump, smiley nurse was holding my wrist.

"Doctor will be here in a jiffy. I think that neck brace will probably come off too. Would you like a drink?"

"Water please," I croaked.

Ten minutes later, the brace was off and I was sitting upright, having the blood washed off my face and a couple of stitches put into a cut just above my hairline. What a fool I felt, I must have hit my head on something sharp, my right hand was grazed and sore.

"You have a visitor," the smiley nurse said and there were the limpid brown eyes surrounded by a head and a body this time. He looked familiar but I couldn't place him. He was dressed in a Paramedics uniform and carried my jacket and boots, which he pushed into the cupboard beside the bed.

"Hello, Laura. A bit concussed I hear."

"Hello?"

"You don't remember me, do you?"

"Should I?"

"We met in Stokesley in the gardening shop. I was a bit cheeky and you sent me off with a flea in my ear," he added helpfully. "See you changed your mind."

"What?"

"No wedding ring," he said, pointing to my hand.

"Mmm, yes," but try as I might I couldn't remember his name. He seemed so familiar and yet... and then it popped into my head. Lawnmowers... shears! Aha, it was all coming back.

"You're Stuart, aren't you? I remember you... Yes, do you work here?"

"Just on the ambulances. What a bit of luck you fell on my shift. I couldn't believe it when I saw it was you. Are you feeling Ok? I'm flattered you remember my name."

My head was thumping by then and I winced with pain as I became aware of other parts of my anatomy that hurt too. My right knee and hand were both bruised.

"I just feel so silly and incredibly tired. What did I hit when I fell?"

"Looks like you missed the step and hit the sill on the outside windows. Must have just caught the corner."

A need to sleep overcame me but I did ask my ambulance man with the lovely eyes to call Diane for me, to explain why I needed her to feed Flo. I managed to give him her number and then I disappeared again into oblivion.

About ten hours later I was fine and wanted to go home but my car was in Darlington. I guessed I would have a ticket on it by then. *Perhaps I could appeal with a doctor's note?* I thought.

After being examined, I was to be allowed to go home if I promised to rest for at least a week. I had to report any dizziness,

91

amnesia or severe head pain immediately. The doctor told me to take pain killers for the headache and rest, so I called Tally and she came straight away to pick me up. She was worried by the way I looked but spoke to the doctor who assured her that I would be fine.

She was unbelievably happy and I wanted to know why. What was happening in her life to make her smile so brightly? How had her Easter holiday been? Having been away and so busy with my job, I hadn't spoken to her since our lunch date.

"Wait until we get you home and settled, and I will tell all," she'd said with a twinkle in her eyes as we drove back home. I could see that it was something really special, but she insisted that it was much more important that I was OK.

My jacket was covered with sludge from the pavement and I needed to soak my aching body in a deep, hot bath. Tally went off and bought us fish and chips, and we sat together, me in my fluffy old dressing gown and Tally looking like she should be at the Ritz, but she kicked off her shoes and settled in with me. Thank God for my dear friend.

"So come on tell me why you're smiling so broadly. Did Mr Michael Parker call off the wedding and fall for you?" I teased. "Yes, he did," she laughed out loud.

"Your joking, Tal! Oh my God, I am so pleased for you." I put my plate to one side and with a mouth full of chips, hugged her as much as my aching body would allow and just knew by her sparkling eyes that she was telling the truth.

"He said that he knew they weren't right for each other and meeting me had confirmed it. He didn't know that I was going at Easter but had told my mother that he wanted to see me again, and she thought it better if he got everything sorted out with his fiancée... ex now of course, so mum didn't tell him and when I got there she told me and... Oh, Laura, I am so happy. He's wonderful. *This* is the 'one'. We're going to wait awhile before we announce our engagement, but we hope to get married early next year, in

Jersey of course because I am going to move there. I only came back yesterday, took a few extra days. Oh, I can't tell you Laura," she'd hardly stopped for breath and then continued, "I have already put my business up for sale and I'm going as soon as I can. Mum and Dad want me to stay with them until we get married. You know they have known him for ages, are practically neighbours, and are so happy for us, they like him so much. We won't get married till next year as Michael has some banking exams to finish. You will come, won't you, Laura?" Her lovely face was alight with excitement.

"Of course, I will come, but God, I will miss you not being here. What will I do without you? You keep me sane. I can always rely on you to make me laugh when I'm low. Still, that's just plain selfish. I'm really thrilled for you."

I was of course delighted for her but how I would miss her exuberance and optimism, her lovely smile and generous personality. I wanted to know more about this 'Mr Paragon of Virtue'.

I heard about how he looked, what he wore, his job, how they planned to have at least three children and where they were going to live. Once started, she couldn't stop, and I was surprised that she hadn't blurted it out in the hospital.

"I didn't know what to expect, Laura, and you looked so pale and fragile. I didn't dare start on about my life and how happy I am. I'm so pleased that you're all right."

Before she left, she tucked me up in bed, promised to organise getting my car back, kissed me at least six times on the good side of my face, made me take some pain killers for my throbbing head, and I slept like a baby again until the next morning when I reported to Miss G-G who was surprisingly kind and sympathetic, and cancelled my following week's appointments.

Then to my absolute delight and surprise, Nick telephoned the next day to inform me that he and Paula had decided to get engaged and

93

were coming to England together so that both Brian and I could meet her. What perfect timing. They were to stay a month from mid-May, first staying with Brian and then travel north to spend two weeks with me and Joe. Paula's parents were coming for a week in June and staying in London with them. After that, they were all going off to Paris and then Italy. Nick wanted me to come to London to see Paula's parents and of course I thought that would be wonderful. I'd have to find a way to get some extra time off.

"I've already told Joe, and he is going to get down to spend time with us too," Nick explained and said he would arrange everything. How exciting it all was, and only a few weeks away. He sounded so happy, but explained that they wouldn't be able to get married until his job finished the following year and then he would move to New York State, Paula's home. He didn't say whether he would stay there.

Apparently Paula's mother was English and came from Kent. Both her parents were killed in a car crash when she was in her early twenties and she had married a guy called Greg soon after and lived in the States for the past twenty-plus years, so was delighted to be coming back for a visit.

All this lovely news and in the space of a week; two weddings to look forward to.

As well as my stitches, I had a huge lump on my forehead and a purple and yellow bruise down one side of my face when Joe came home for the weekend.

"What in heaven's name have you been up to? Why didn't you tell me? I would have come straight down," he said, as he dropped his bag in the hall.

"I'm OK."

"Mother, you look terrible."

"Thanks son. Actually it looks worse than it is. I had a fall in Darlington, only two stitches," I said turning to go into the kitchen to put the kettle on but the phone rang. "Go and make the tea, Joe, while I get this." It was Stuart.

"Hi, Laura. Just sweet-talked your neighbour into giving me your number. I had her number for the cat, remember? But not yours and I just wanted to know that you are OK."

"Thanks, Stuart. I am fine now, just look a bit grim, according to my son."

"Oh, is he there? Good, I'm glad you're not on your own. I found a scarf in the wagon, thought it must be yours, red and sort of stripy?"

"Yes, that's mine. I hadn't even missed it."

"Can I pop it round now? I live in Stokesley."

"Of course. Come and have a cuppa with us and you can explain to Joe what happened." I gave him my address.

He arrived and grimaced when he saw my face. He held out my scarf.

"Could have been worse, I guess, but he's right you do look... erm... pretty grim."

"OK, no need to tell me. I do have a mirror." I laughed as he made a face. "Come on in, the tea's ready."

Ten minutes later we were all sitting in the kitchen and Stuart was making Joe laugh by telling him how I was like sleeping beauty with blood running down my face, and how getting me to hospital was so nerve-wracking because I wouldn't keep my eyes open.

"I was unconscious and concussed," I laughed. Stuart smiled and asked Joe about his course and what he wanted to do. Joe paused when he mentioned Australia again instinctively knowing how much

I would hate him going back. Joe asked Stuart about his job, and I sat and listened sipping my tea and wondering how I could have turned down those lovely brown eyes. He'd been a Paramedic most of his working life and enjoyed it. He hesitated when Joe asked about his family. A widower, he said, no children, then changed the subject quickly and easily as if that was what he always did.

"I have two lovely nieces," he said. "Twelve and sixteen who live nearby so I see them every weekend."

He commented on my garden and told me that if I ever wanted any help, he had free time off shift. He liked gardening and grew all his own vegetables. "I could plant some for you," he said with a smile.

Mmm. I thought, *might just take you up on that, Mr Paramedic.*

Before he left, he asked me if he could call again, just call, didn't mention a date or going for a drink or anything else, and I was a bit disappointed, I must admit. He was such pleasant company and I would have liked to have got to know him better.

Perhaps if I took him up on his offer to help me in the garden?

***

CHAPTER 11

Time went so fast. The weather improved, I got back to work, arranged my time off and cleaned the house till it shone, and before I knew it Nick was on his way back with Paula. I'd spoken to her briefly on the telephone, and she was excited and apprehensive about meeting us all. I'd planned all sorts of outings and would try to make her as welcome as I could. I'd even revamped Nick's old room with Joe's help, putting away all his childhood stuff, bought new bedding for his old double bed, and made it look smart and welcoming. I had no doubt that was what they would want. I was so excited at the thought of having both my boys home together, I filled the freezer with tempting dishes, even though I knew we would be out most of the time. I'd invited Tally, Teresa and Vic to dinner at the May bank holiday weekend so had made spicy Thai fish cakes, paté, a lamb casserole plus a huge fish pie (Nick's favourite), a few cakes and pastries and a summer pudding.

I thought I would invite Stuart too but realised I hadn't asked him for his number. I hoped that he would call before they came.

Just over a week, later he did and I was happy to see him again.

He arrived one sunny evening when I'd just got in from work, and he pushed a small bunch of freesias towards me. Smiling, I took them and held them to my nose.

"I hope you don't mind," he said sheepishly. "I haven't got an excuse this time, just thought I would see if you looked any better… And, yes, you do… a bit."

"Funny, ha ha. I'm completely back to normal."

"Right."

So I invited him in for a glass of wine and we spent the next hour or so chatting. Our conversation was light-hearted. He had a way of making things sound amusing, and I liked the way his face crinkled when he smiled.

"How long have you been divorced?" he asked.

"Since just after I first met you," I'd laughed. "I hadn't got used to the idea then. I was a bit scared of other men and well… I'm still learning how to be on my own and date again. How long have you been widowed?"

His eyes flickered away from me, and he said flatly, "Over three years now." He avoided my gaze and bent to tickle Flo as she wound herself around his legs. I could see by his expression that he found it difficult to talk about, so I said, "My eldest son Nick and his new fiancée Paula will be here next week and for the May Bank holiday so, at the weekend I'm having some friends and the family to dinner. Would you like to come?"

"Sorry, no I can't. I'm working all that weekend, late shift."

"Oh that's a shame." *Damn,* I thought. "Perhaps another time then. Can I have your number and I'll call you if we do it again before they go?"

"Sure," he said, and dropped a card in my fruit bowl. "Must go. Lovely to see you again Laura." And off he went.

What was the matter with me? He obviously doesn't fancy me like he did last year. He seemed very keen then. He left without suggesting another visit or a date again.

Teresa called in later that day and I told her about Stuart's brief visit.

"Did he ask you out this time?"

"No, What's wrong with me?"

"Why not? There's nothing wrong with you."

"Hell, I don't know. He doesn't respond to any of my flirting and I even asked him to our dinner party and he *says* he's working. I think he's gone off me."

"But he comes back... I bet he'll be here again soon. Worry not, he likes you, but something is holding him back. You could ask him."

"I don't think I could," I said as I recalled his off handedness as he left. Too many other things to think about anyway, and I couldn't wait to meet my forthcoming daughter-in-law.

On arrival at Heathrow they called me, saying they were tired after the flight but Nick was renting a car and going to his dad's for two nights and then driving north. I'd arranged to have three weeks off work and was beside myself with excitement. Joe was coming home, but just for a one week. Tally phoned and told me that Michael was coming to England on business and staying over the May bank holiday. Could he come to dinner with us the following weekend?

"Of course, my darling. We want to meet him. The boys will love to see you too. Teresa's intrigued that it's all happened so fast and will be over the moon to meet the man who has finally tamed you. Warn him he'll be thoroughly vetted by your very best friends?"

"Oh, yes he's expecting that," she laughed. "He does know about my past and Mark, so he will not be phased by anything... I hope. Can't wait to see the boys too. Oh, Laura, life is so good at the moment. I can't tell you how happy I am."

"I know, and I'm so pleased for you both."

May is England's most beautiful month, I always think. The garden looked glorious, flowers at their best and the shrubs and trees blowsy with blossoms. The weather has given up its April showers for blowy, mild sunny days. With the heady scent of hawthorn blossom and cow parsley decorating every roadside and hedgerow there is the lurking promise of summer in the air.

Joe arrived on the twentieth and Nick and Paula got to us on the twenty-first. They were both glowing with the happiness of love and youth. Paula, a slight, pretty, very American blonde, so perfectly complimented Nick's tall, dark good looks. She was nervous and excited, smiled a lot and her wide blue eyes lit up whenever their future was mentioned. Chaos reigned for the first twenty-four hours or so, so much to talk about, to catch up with but I watched my boys with such pride and when we were all together, I couldn't think of anything in the world that could be more satisfying. Brian's absence from our family didn't seem to be much of a problem for the boys, they were so much more grown up now. Paula fitted in well and although I found she did little other than gaze lovingly at Nick while I bustled around organising and serving food and drink, she was a thoroughly likeable young woman.

We all went to York for the day and I was reminded of my first meeting with Gordon. No regrets though, and I was so happy to be here with my family. Like all Americans, Paula enthused over the wonderful architecture and history of the place, took a million photographs and smiled constantly.

"Oh, I would love to live here, Nick," she sighed.

Nick hugged her and said, "It's unlikely that I would get a good enough job here, darling."

We stopped for coffee at 'Betty's' and lunched by the river then took a cruise trip. The sparkling sun on the water cast a glorious light over us all. The boys drank too much and behaved like a couple of teenagers again, teasing and play punching each other, much to Paula and my amusement. We linked arms and watched as they joked and jostled each other, obviously pleased to be together again after so long apart.

The following day I took them all to Whitby, did the steps and the lovely alleyways. We bought old photographs and Whitby jet jewellery then had fish and chips overlooking the little harbour.

Paula was subdued that day and told me quietly that she had pre-menstrual problems and that it would probably be better not to go out the following day as she knew her period was about to start and she suffered terrible pains.

"Will you be OK by the weekend?" I asked, worried that she would be unwell for the planned dinner party.

"Oh, yes. It only lasts a couple of days. I have some medication for it. Can we have a day at home?" she asked sweetly.

"Of course, perhaps the boys would like a day out together and we can stay at home and get to know each other." I suggested somewhat concerned by her serious expression.

So the next day the boys went off to a rugby club and met up with some old mates from school, and poor Paula as expected, lay in bed till noon and came down looking strained and pale. I smiled at her and gestured for her to sit down.

"Do you want some tea or coffee?" I asked, busy making a fruit salad for supper and Paula plonked her self down and put her head in her hands.

"Coffee please," she replied looking downhearted. "Laura... I think I have a problem... I'm going for some tests when I get home and my doctor thinks I might have endometriosis. I am really worried because it prevents pregnancy and I know Nick wants a family eventually." Her eyes filled with tears. "There is treatment for it, I know, but I *am* concerned. Think they laser the bad bits off or something but I'm so scared about it."

"Oh, Paula. You are very young. I'm sure it is something that can be sorted." I put my arm across her shoulder.

"I haven't told Nick... I'm afraid to tell him. Do you think I should?" she asked, and her eyes were damp as she looked up at me.

"Yes I think that you should. Talk about everything. One of our problems... that is Brian and I... was that we never really talked. I don't think even after all our years of marriage we knew each other at all and it's because we didn't talk. We didn't communicate how we felt or why we felt it, what was wrong or anything at all. We just jiggled on through life and never questioned whether we were happy or not, and then Sophie came along and... well I'm sure you know what happened. Nick loves you and he will be supportive, I'm sure."

She smiled. "OK, I will talk to him but I'm worried. He does so want a family. I can't even tell my parents. They can't wait to have grandchildren." Holding her arms across her stomach, her forehead creased and obviously in pain, she asked, "Can I have a bath? It sometimes helps the cramps."

"Of course. Use some of my essential oils." She picked up her coffee and said, "Thanks, Laura," and trotted off up the stairs again.

It was several hours later that she came back down looking refreshed by which time I was tired having done all the preparation for the evening meal and a few extra things for the freezer, put out the washing, fed Flo, watered the garden pots, done a bit of weeding in the rockery. I was ready to sit down with a gin and tonic.

"Better?" I asked.

"Mmm... I'm a bit peckish now. Can I make a sandwich?"

"Help yourself. Get a gin and tonic too if you want one. I'm going to sit in the garden for a bit. We have to enjoy the sun while we've got it here, you know," I said determinedly pushing open the French doors, which led on to my small patio that was bathed in late afternoon sunshine.

As we sat together and sipped our drinks, I warmed to my son's choice of partner. She was vague and pretty, and dressed in a casual, almost indifferent way. Her jewellery was small and delicate and on her tiny feet she wore skimpy sandals. She wore little makeup and laughed warmly and easily, her cheeks rounding as she smiled so she looked like a small child. She was still studying as a dental nurse, but had a sensible attitude toward life and family, and was in her own way determined to make my son happy. We talked again briefly about her forthcoming tests and she promised me that she would be open with Nick about the possible consequences.

The boys returned home in time for dinner and Paula put on a good act about how our day had been but not a word about our conversation or her painful period. Because they had had such a good day, nothing more was said at all.

They all went off the next day together and did a tour of the area, showing Paula where they went to school and the house we lived in when they were small. They climbed Roseberry Topping and went to the James Cook museum whilst I stayed at home catching up with some paper work and as the sun was shining, did a bit of tidying in the garden. Tally called and asked what time to come to the dinner party and enthused again about Michael and how lovely life was.

"OK, I'm bored now. Just want to meet this paragon of perfect virtue," I laughed at her. "How's the sale of the business going?"

"Not at all. I think it might take longer than I expected, but never mind, Michael comes over quite regularly so we will take our time. See you then, darling. We'll bring some good wine. Michael is a bit of a connoisseur."

"Of course he is. Would we expect anything else?" We both giggled and said goodbye.

The weekend arrived and I spent time organising the food, the table and the seating. I couldn't wait to get all my lovely people together. Life felt so incredibly wonderful that I hoped it would never end. Sadly and inevitably, things change all the time, and soon Nick and Paula would be gone, and Tally would leave for Jersey. Joe would be back at university. Me? Perhaps, I would go back to the dating site.

On the evening of our dinner party, Tally and Michael arrived first. Tally looked fabulous in a flattering emerald dress, her dark curls framing her happy face. Michael was everything she said he was; tall dark and handsome, incredibly well dressed with that sort of immaculate, well-coordinated look that comes from money and breeding. He was charming beyond words and I could see instantly why Tally had fallen for him. He took my outstretched hand as he said, "Good evening, Laura. So pleased to meet you."

"And you, Michael. You're still a bit of a surprise to us all."

"So I am told. You're not going to give me a grilling, are you?"

"Not me," I smiled, holding up my hands, "but Teresa might. She's very protective of Tally, but we do want to get to know you. I'm so happy for you both."

He grinned, handed me a bottle of expensive wine, then turned to Tally and took her hand and it was so obvious how much he adored her. She glowed with happiness.

Nick came galloping down the stairs and to Michael's surprise, lifted Tally off her feet in a great bear hug. She'd always been one of his favourite people and as a teenager he'd had an almighty crush on her.

"God, how tall you are Nicky boy." she laughed.

"You're as gorgeous as ever, Tal. Have you met my fiancée, Paula, yet?"

"No, just arrived, this is *my* fiancé Michael," she said turning so that Nick could shake Michael's hand.

Taking his hand, Nick said. "You're a lucky bloke Michael. She's one of the best."

With Tally beaming from ear to ear, Nick led them off to meet Paula.

Teresa and Vic arrived late, and by then, we all had drinks, and Joe, Nick and Michael were chatting about educational grants and bank loans. Apparently Michael was involved in the banking world and specialised in helping the young get their finances in order. Paula and Tally were deep in conversation, heads together and laughing, probably talking about weddings.

Teresa's first question to me was, "What's Michael like then?"

"Lovely," I replied, as she dropped her coat in my arms. "Go on… go in and meet him." Off she scooted into the lounge to find him.

Vic handed me a bottle of brandy and winked. "Knowing her she'll give him a hard time, but her bark is worse than her bite. It's taken me a while to find out but she's marshmallow underneath."

I hung Teresa's coat in the hall cupboard and turning smiled, "I know, that's why I love her."

Taking his arm and leading him towards my now-noisy lounge I said, "Come and meet my lot, Vic. Can't tell you how lovely it is to have them all here. How are yours by the way?"

"Good… yes, very good," he said, and I introduced him to everybody. Confident, happy Teresa had introduced herself and was already laughing with Tally and Paula.

"Michael, he's bloody gorgeous," she whispered as I joined them. "Just look at him. He looks like a cross between Tom Cruise and Johnny Depp. A taller version though… Fandabidoozie. I have a

feeling he's just what Tal needs, but is he too good to be true?"
Tally laughed and shook her head.

"Haven't found any cracks yet. He treats me like a princess
and is incredible in the... *you know what.*" She glanced at Paula not
sure how she would react, but Paula laughed with us, and Tally went
on. "I can't believe how I could ever have thought I was happy, you
know before... with Mark. I feel as if my life has just begun. I am
so totally, totally in love with him. I just can't believe my luck."

Teresa, Paula and I were all carried along with her happiness.

"You deserve the best," I said, and hugged my lovely friend,
and then took off into the kitchen while they all got to know each
other. I'd decided on the Thai fishcakes, the lamb casserole and the
summer pudding but still had all the vegetables to cook and sauces to
make.

After a few minutes Teresa popped her head around the door. "Need
some help, hon?"

"Just stir this sauce for me, will you? I need to make some
custard. Well, what do you think?"

"Michael or Paula?"

"Both."

"Michael's divine and I think he'll be perfect for Tal. He has
everything her other blokes didn't... if you know what I mean.
Handsome *and* strong *and* intelligent. He will look after her too, I'm
sure. Paula, I'm not sure about, she is sweet, but a bit too simpering
for me and... I don't know... I suppose she might be shy, and she is
very young. Perhaps she'll grow on me."

"Good for Nick though, don't you think? He likes that sort of
fair, feminine type and I think she has her head screwed on. She
loves my boy and that's what matters to me."

"Yes, obviously she   does."

106

"What do you know about endometriosis? Don't say anything to anyone because Nick doesn't know, but Paula thinks she is going to need treatment for it."

"Oh, horrible thing, endometriosis." Teresa appeared to consider for a moment and then added, "It's due to the over production of oestrogen in the body. Not a lot helps but surgery can, sometimes. She needs to see a nutritionist because it can be helped enormously with diet. In most cases it reduces fertility... Did you know that?"

"Yes, Paula told me. She's really worried."

"This sauce is cooked. What shall I do with it?"

I handed her a dish and said, "Don't say anything, will you?"

She shook her head. I knew Teresa well enough to know that she was very discreet but I couldn't risk Nick finding out before Paula had a chance to tell him.

We carried the first course through, and I put the cooked vegetables and lamb casserole in my trusty hostess trolley, which hadn't been used since before Brian left.

Everyone enjoyed the food and the conversation flowed well and I was delighted with the whole evening. I sat next to Vic and it was the first time I'd really appreciated what an interesting person he was. He told me about his life in the army and how he studied law in his spare time to become a solicitor. At first glance he looked rather staid and boring. He seemed like a man permanently dressed for being outdoors with checked shirts and usually corduroys, always brown. He had a good body shape with a thin, beaky face and his dark hair worn rather long, given his profession. First impressions can be so wrong, as we soon discovered, by his rather cryptic humour and ability to mimic accents and people. He did a rather amusing impression of Edna Everage which made us all laugh. Paula wasn't quite sure what was going on but nevertheless grinned at our amusement.

Joe got out his guitar after dinner and he, Nick and Paula sang a few popular country songs. In the small space of my lounge, Teresa showed us a bit of line dancing, and we all had a go except Vic who said he had two left feet when it came to dancing.

"He has too," Teresa panted.

Even Michael had a try, not very successfully, but then he sat and watched as Tally moved her lovely body to the music, dark hair swinging. I noticed how his eyes followed her as she swayed. It was full of love and pride. I could see so much affection and happiness around me that night and I, once again, appreciated how lucky I was.

***

CHAPTER 12

We visited Dad in Leeds and he excelled himself with his enthusiasm for Paula who was quiet and passive, and I think Nick must have warned her about his chauvinistic attitudes, as she played along charmingly. He congratulated Nick on his choice of a wife but expressed his concern about them being so young.

"We're not getting married just yet, Gramps," Nick said, "and I'll be nearly twenty-six by then, much older than when you got married to Gran. Nineteen weren't you?"

"Ah, yes, the war, you know." He sighed, making Nick and Paula laugh.

Too soon, the two weeks had passed, Joe had gone back to Uni and we were off to London to meet Paula's parents. Nick drove us down to the Strand Palace, an old comfortable, central hotel where we were all staying. Greg and Marianne Bradlaw had arrived the previous day, and were well rested when we met them in the bar of the Savoy. We thought it would be rather grand to have afternoon tea there. And it was!

Greg had a look of Burt Lancaster, but was rather overweight with a set of glowing white teeth, so obviously false, but nevertheless gave his whole face a youthful appearance. Marianne was just an older version of Paula, with soft blonde hair and the same blue eyes. They were both so pleased to be in England and beamed at all the plans Nick had made: The Tower of London, Madam Tussauds, Buckingham Palace, the Tate Gallery, the Natural History Museum, as Greg was manager of several art and antiquity museums in New York, and a visit to the theatre to see 'Phantom of the Opera'. In between, Marianne and I shopped, and had our hair done at Vidal Sassoon in Knightsbridge.

Such extravagance! I knew I would have to be frugal over the coming months, but I wasn't really worried, as my commission at ArtLovers Magazine had almost doubled.

The week flew by. We collapsed every evening in various eating places around Convent Garden or Soho, one night in Camden town after scouring the market where Nick bought me an early birthday present; a lovely silver pendant with a large quartz crystal cut in the shape of a long teardrop. Another night was Leicester Square where there was a brilliant jazz band and the food was a mix of Caribbean and French. Unfortunately the weather was awful with endless rain and we all bought bright colourful plastic Macs from a street market so we didn't have to carry umbrellas. With a sense of fun, Greg had bartered with the stallholder and we got the five for the price of four. I had a brilliant green one, Nick and Greg yellow and orange, Paula in red and Marianne in a rather gaudy violet so we looked like a little family of plastic people from a children's television programme scuttling along and giggling with each other whenever we got stared at. We all laughed at the 'English summer'.

Greg insisted on treating us to a special evening out on our last night together.

So we dressed up, me in my honey chiffon that brought back memories of Luis --*Where was he now?* -- Marianne in her new Donna Karan outfit. We took a taxi to avoid the rain and went to Marco Pierre White's restaurant 'Wheelers of St James'.

"I guess next time we see you will be at the wedding, Laura?" said the slightly inebriated Greg as we finished dinner and were sipping our Irish coffees.

"Oh, yes. Have you two decided on a date yet?" I asked looking at Paula. I caught the slightly fearful look in her glance and then she dropped her eyes and replied, "No, not yet." She'd obviously not told Nick or her family about her forthcoming tests. I wondered what their reaction would be and why she hadn't at least talked to her mother about it.

"It'll probably be next summer, so start saving, Mum." Nick winked as he replied. I pulled my eyes away from Paula and hoped all would be well. If Nick loved her as he said, I was sure they'd be able to adopt babies if they couldn't have their own. Paula had told me quietly one afternoon that it was relatively easy in the States, but she was not sure whether Nick would agree.

'Talk to him,' I'd said, 'and don't leave it too long.' I knew she would in her own good time and was sure that the wedding would go ahead as planned.

Marianne smiled and tapped the table excitedly. "Summer or fall is best so we can have it in the garden at our place. It'll be lovely. Plenty of space for a marquee and a floral walkway from the house. Oh darling I can't wait," she gushed.

Paula lifted her eyes at that point and smiled at her mother who continued. "Let's think now… the garden is at it's best in June and we can get Greg's parents there then. They travel a lot, you know. Even your cousin Jaynie's twins will be old enough to come by June next year. *And* we have plenty of room -- seven bedrooms -- everyone can stay with us. All Nick's family too," Marianne added enthusiastically.

Not Brian and Sophie, I thought. *I'm not quite ready for that.*

"You'll stay with us won't you, Laura, and Joe too, of course?" Marianne asked, turning to me to see why I was hesitating. "Oh," she said, clearly realising what was going through my mind. "We can sort that later."

"Thanks, Marianne, I'm sure that will be lovely and yes, we *will* sort it later."

She smiled. "We've all got on so well and I have to say what a pleasure this week has been, hasn't it, Greg?"

111

"Sure has… a great pleasure. I don't know when I enjoyed myself more."

"You will stay with us won't you, Laura?" Marianne asked again.

"Of course I will." It would probably be a grand affair as Greg and Marianne appeared affluent and generous, and obviously approved of Nick.

The next day I got my train back home and said a tearful farewell to Nick and his new family. They were off to Kent to see Marianne's one remaining relative in England, a brother who still lived in the family home. Then they were flying to Paris the following morning so with promises of calls and e-mails we parted and I felt optimistic and happy about their future together. I liked the Bradlaw family immensely.

The next week passed quickly with lots to do both at work and in the garden where flowers needed dead heading and the lawn mowing. All the rain had made the grass long and green. Bright poppies, aquilegia, sweet peas and petunias jostled for space and my terrace was full of pots overflowing with pansies and pinks. I loved my garden and found immense pleasure in the feel of the earth between my fingertips and the satisfaction of clearing the weeds that had spread out of all proportion that they threatened to strangle my flowers. I filled my bird feeders and enjoyed the antics of those who came to visit, especially my resident robins and blackbirds. With my little stone bird bath cleaned and topped up with fresh water, I felt a sense of satisfaction and with the spell of fine weather sat on my terrace with a G&T and 'smelled the roses.'

I felt exceedingly happy with life.

I saw Stuart one hot day whilst shopping in Stokesley. He looked pleased to see me and we had a coffee together outside a local bistro. I thought I looked rather cheerful and summery in a pair of white trousers and a pastel blue shirt, my hair newly trimmed, and with the pampering of Vidal Sassoon products, looked and smelt good.

Stuart was tanned and looked attractive too in beige shorts and a chocolate-coloured, short-sleeved shirt. It complimented those limpid brown eyes perfectly. He had been to the farmers market and carried a bag overflowing with plants. I told him all about Nick and Paula, the fun we had had at my dinner party, our trip to London and how much I missed them now they were gone.

"You have had a busy time," he smiled.

Beside those lovely crinkly eyes which were hidden by a smart pair of sunglasses, I noticed what a wide, kissable mouth he had and I moved a little closer to him and tilting my head, with my hand under my chin and said in my most alluring voice, "So, what have you been doing since I last saw you then?"

"Not a lot," he said, ignoring my flirting. "I lead rather a boring life compared to you."

OK, I thought, *that's it. I'm not trying anymore. You obviously don't fancy me like I fancy you… I am making a fool of myself here. We'll just be friends if that's what you want.*

"Why are you frowning at me?" He leaned forward and placed his hand over mine. Just for a moment I thought he might be responding to me but then he said, "I am going to Tunisia for a holiday with my sister's family when the girls break up from school, around about the tenth July I think… I'm looking forward to that. That won't be boring for sure, they are a couple of live-wires."

It was my birthday on July tenth, and possibly the second on my own. Back to the dating site then!

I updated my profile, adding that I would only reply to those who lived in the North East, had photos on the site, and who were in my age range, then I hoped for the best. As I hadn't been on the site for so long, there were several unread messages. I was getting better at sorting the really interesting ones. I deleted anything that was over sexed, too clever, too boring or too far away.

Amongst my messages, there was one that introduced Simon D, 44 from Great Ayton, 5'8", a businessman with one son living at home with him and a daughter living with his mother close by. His profile was funny and edgy, with a bit of poetry thrown in, and a liking for antiques and jazz. It suggested a light-hearted, cheerful person and I decided to message him.

Happy and chatty, I thought later when I called him. *Nothing fancy or pretentious about him.* He told me that he was basically lazy, letting his brother Ian run the family business, which was a factory in Stockton making specialised doors and windows.

On a sunny afternoon, we met outside 'The Royal Oak' in Great Ayton. He was leaning on a post, smoking a cigarette and smiled broadly when he saw me approaching.

"Laura, what a lovely smile you have. So pleased to meet you." He flicked his cigarette aside and, with both hands, took my outstretched hand and shook it firmly.

Having introduced ourselves, we walked across to the village green opposite. Sitting together in the late afternoon sun, we chatted and laughed easily. I felt quite relaxed and happy in his company.

"Shall we walk? I could get some bread to feed the ducks?" he asked after a while. I nodded and we set off. He popped into a small bakery close by and came out with a huge bag of rolls and buns. We walked by the river and the sunlight danced on the rippling water, the overhanging willows whispering in the gentle breeze.

114

Ducks came from all directions as Simon began to throw pieces of the bread, and he slipped several times on the bank trying to throw to the farthest bird. He chortled as the ducks jostled for the best place. His mood was infectious, and I found myself laughing with him. His air of over-indulged self-confidence was only a spit away from arrogance. Jewish, broad bodied and paunchy, his whiskery face was tanned and crinkled with laughter lines. He had a receding hairline and lovely blue eyes. He exuded good energy and *bon vivant*. His clothes were a little on the scruffy side but nevertheless, he looked like a man who could well afford not to make an effort. His disgracefully scuffed brogues, had a Jermyn Street handmade look about them that I immediately recognised as Brian's father had all his shoes custom made there.

Simon and I had a drink and a bar meal in the local pub and I felt quite relaxed about going back to his house for coffee. He was an utter gentleman and as I left, he kissed my fingertips and laughed as we arranged to meet again soon.

After a couple of dates, I came to the conclusion that Simon was just what I needed; a completely uncomplicated, a fun loving, lazy bastard who called me a 'sexy minx' and bought me sweet little presents. He let me be myself so that I could relax with him and he was good company, and listened to my experiences in my job and about my sons and my boring marriage. He was sympathetic and supportive, and hugged me when I got a bit emotional.

On my forty-second birthday, he took me to an expensive restaurant so I wasn't on my own after all. After presenting me with an enormous bunch of roses and some bubble bath, I felt thoroughly spoilt. We ate lobster and crème brûlée, and drank champagne and he guffawed when presented with the bill so I offered to pay my share.

"Oh, no," he laughed, "birthdays only come once a year."

His frequent outbursts of laughter were somewhat loud and infectious but never irritating. I liked the way he laughed easily, responded to things that amused him and always showed his pleasure when I took his hand or told him something interesting. His house on the outskirts of Great Ayton was huge and rambling. He had a cleaner called Mrs Mills and a gardener called Ken. He went to work only when absolutely necessary.

"I know my brother Ian is far more competent than I am and I don't really think I make much of a contribution at all, but nevertheless I get a comfortable wage, and know that at some point I will have to justify it," he told me between puffs of his Benson and Hedges.

"I'm an extremely happy man and now I have met you Laura... how good can it get?"

He spent much of his time buying and selling a few antiques, collecting clocks and his house was filled with them; wonderful examples of old and new craftsmanship, tick-ticking away in every room. He loved auctions and second-hand shops and I enjoyed our weekends together when we went to house and antique sales.

I met his teenage son, Ashley, who was a bright clever lad, a typical teenager who had a love / hate relationship with his dad and was busy studying for his A levels. He came and went in a seemingly random way and when he was home, spent most of his time in his own two rooms at the far end of the house. Simon's nine-year-old daughter, Amelia, stayed every other weekend and I kept away when she was around, as she was very jealous of any other female within a hundred yards of her dad.

Simon became a confidant and friend as well as an enthusiastic lover. His kisses were sexy and usually left me with whisker burn, and sex with Simon was spontaneous and enthusiastic. He pounced with the enthusiasm and clumsiness of a Labrador puppy, always with good humour and bounced on top of me calling me silly names. His idea of foreplay was ticklish and sloppy, but his enthusiastic fucking left me sweating and panting. Satisfied, he'd cuddle up to me and reckoned our sexual romp was 'superlative'. He was well-endowed and I found it enjoyable and generally satisfying, somewhat amusing at times, after all who could resist such a cute, cuddly puppy? Simon's good nature always made up for anything else that was lacking. He loved to stroke my naked body and sucked on my breasts until they were sore, muttering, 'Lolly, my lovely little Lolly,' and he made me feel cherished and appreciated.

He smoked non-stop, dropping his ash into any receptacle available. His eating habits were interesting too; a convert to vegetarianism he did occasionally eat chicken or bacon and then felt guilty about it because of his religion and his love of animals. Most of his meals were microwaved or produced by Mrs Mills.

If it wasn't for the fact that he was so lacking in any sort of drive or ambition, I think our relationship would have continued, but he began to slow me down just when I was really beginning to feel that I was doing well in my job. He never wanted to get up in the morning and tugged me back under the bedclothes towards his huge early morning erection, when I was trying to get ready for work. He was always late, laughed at everything, and was so good-natured but I really didn't like his lifestyle that relied on other people to do his work all the time. Mrs Mills was at his house every day picking up his clothes, cleaning and cooking for him. Ken worked his socks off in the huge garden.

"Couldn't you at least mow the lawn sometimes?" I asked, despairingly one day after seeing Simon loll on the couch all afternoon, watching the rugby.

"Why would I when I have Ken? You don't keep a dog and bark yourself."

"Because the fresh air and exercise would do you good, and anyway you are just getting lazier and lazier, *and* fat. What do you ever do that involves moving faster than a slug?"

"I fuck you baby," he said with a grin, then leapt up and tickled my ribs. That's a bit faster than any old slug, hey my little minx?" Although he made me laugh, I was beginning to find him irritating and his constant smoking gave me a chesty cough and at times his breath was like an old cowshed.

Time to move on... Short and definitely sweet, but not for me.

I'd heard from Nick that week that Paula had discussed her problem with him when they were in Italy, but she still hadn't told her mother, who was apparently very keen to have grandchildren as soon as possible.

"Thanks for talking to Paula, Mum. She really did appreciate being able to tell you," he said, "but the tests don't look good and she is considering having some surgery in a few months time. In the meantime she's going to try a few other options; improved diet, reflexology, and that sort of thing. We're going to try everything."

It sounded like they were still going to go ahead with their plans for a summer wedding the following year and I was so pleased that Nick had taken the news so well.

Maria had also called that week and told me that both she and Hamish were well and that Luis had met a Canadian lady who he was seeing regularly and seemed very happy. He was now considering a job in Vancouver.

Let's hope he 'glue's' with this one. I thought, smiling at the memory of our little fling on the terrace, although I was pleased for him.

I'd been really busy that week and had all the contents of my workbag spread out on the kitchen table and was trying to catch up

118

with my paperwork when Stuart called in with some vegetables from his garden.

"Lettuce, green beans, tomatoes and courgettes." He plonked them on my kitchen table.

How kind he is, I thought. *I wonder what's prompted this?*

"Thanks, Stuart. How very thoughtful of you."

He stayed for about half an hour, told me all about his holiday in Tunisia with his sister and nieces, drank my coffee and I even made him a toasted sandwich, but he still didn't suggest a date. He did ask about Joe, and whether I was busy and where had I been. I didn't tell him about Simon. I tried flirting with him again, asked him about his garden and his job and although he answered politely, he almost completely ignored me and then he left. I gave up wondering why he didn't ask me out.

The next evening, I was just about to set off for my yoga class when I got the phone call from Ed. I was late and I'd answered the phone with my Yoga mat tucked under one arm and my keys and bag in the other. My heart leapt and I dropped my mat on the floor as I heard him sobbing loudly. I couldn't make out what he was saying at first.

"What... what is it, Ed?"

"I don't know how to tell you Laura... I know you were fond of him."

"What... Ed, what," I yelled. "What has happened?"

"Gordon... he's dead... been found dead at Jan and Dave's," he sobbed. "They're in the States, you know... he was house-sitting the cats. A huge overdose. Don't know what he took but he was into all sorts... Oh, Laura, it has scared the shit out of me."

For a moment, I was speechless with shock. All I could think was, *he didn't like cats.* I stood with my hand over my mouth, tears rushing to my eyes and tipping down my cheeks. I couldn't take it in. Gordon was dead.

"Was it deliberate, do you think?" I whispered, thinking of our conversation in his cottage about death and dying. Ed stopped sobbing and was sniffing loudly.

"No, I shouldn't think so… He *was* fine when I saw him last week but he had got into it bad, Laura. There will be an inquest of course… Thought you would want to know. He told me you knew about the drugs and that was why you left him."

"It was one reason but I didn't think he had such a problem with it… with the drugs. He *was* depressing and bloody moody at times… They went up and down very quickly, his moods," I said softly, remembering the worst of them and how quickly they changed after his 'medication'.

"He thought the stuff helped, but I think it got worse...made it worse. Definitely, and he went too far," Ed babbled on. "He started in Singapore you know. He worked with Dave there. Jeez, Laura he was my best friend and I couldn't stop him… Told him he was doing too much. Even his family were fed up with him."

"I didn't know that. Who found him, Ed?"

"Henry and Milly. They were going to spend the evening together to celebrate their pregnancy… Oh god, I have to tell his children," he said as he started sobbing again.

"You'll you let me know about the inquest and funeral won't you?"

How dreadful that this had happened to such a basically decent man. He had been kind to me, but I had realised that there was something wrong, but never really imagined that it was so bad that he could kill himself. What on earth was going on in his head that he could that he could dismiss himself from life so completely?

What deep trouble he must have been in, what terrible damage he must have caused himself?

Ed had got off the phone still crying and promised to keep me informed. I didn't think I would go to the funeral as I hadn't really known him well and never met any of his family, but I would send some flowers. I had been fond of Gordon and although it hadn't lasted long we'd had some good times together.

***

CHAPTER 13

It was less than a week later that I received a message from 'Benton Blaze' 48, from Newcastle, a Scorpio over 6 ' and looking for *dating only.*

Hello, Lolly. Lovely smile and your lips look like they need to be kissed.

Ha! A cheeky one. I smiled and read on.

I'm on business close to you next week. Want to meet up. Ben

Mmm, straight to the point and looking at his profile I was attracted to the idea of an adventurous free thinker who liked what I liked.

I am looking for a lively, fun loving lady who will appreciate a caring, sensitive guy who loves life and lives it to the full. I travel a great deal, am adventurous and free thinking. Love fast cars, good wine, gardens, history, theatre and petite brunettes!

So message him I did. How could I not? I'm fun loving, caring, travel a lot and like the theatre and good wine. I could be described as petite, I'm 5'4'' and definitely brunette. Perfect!

As I drove into the pub car park where we had arranged to meet it was raining hard but I noticed him straight away, he couldn't be missed. He was standing beside his blue BMW holding a large umbrella. The spaces close to his car were full so I had to pull in on the other side of the car park. He watched me park my car and strolled towards me. I could see him in my wing mirror as I collected my bag and gloves. His body was lean and he moved with a fluid grace. I took my time, undid my seat belt watching him moving across the car park. He was expensively dressed in a casual suit, topped with a dark cashmere coat. He had a confident and rather sardonic look. By the time I stepped out of my car, he was beside it smiling. Yes, confident, intimate and unmistakably sexual.

"Good evening, Laura. I'm Ben."

He was gorgeous and I smiled a 'hello' as he leaned down to kiss my cheek. He was at least 6'3" with grey streaked dark hair with amazing blue eyes. He was definitely older than his profile had said and moved into my personal space as if he had the right. He held the umbrella over me as I shivered in the cold wind, then took my elbow and guided me toward the door of the hotel and then to a seat in the corner of the bar. He had obviously been there before.

"Wine?"

"Red please, yes."

It was unusually cold and wet for the beginning of September and having deposited my damp coat and gloves, I sat by the lovely log fire and warmed my chilly hands.

When he returned with the wine, he sat so close to me I was aware straight away of the warmth of him. I felt comfortable with it and his wide mouth and sexy hooded eyes gave me a tingling sensation that seemed to spread over my whole body. He laid his arm across the chair behind me and I found myself responding to his closeness with a smile, and I guess I was encouraging him.

"So pleased to meet you, Laura. How are you finding MakingDatesForYou? Have you had any really good matches yet?"

"A few, yes, but no one special." I decided not to tell him about Gordon or Simon. "I'm enjoying meeting people and getting out. How about you?"

"Don't you get out much then?" he asked ignoring my question.

"I didn't before, no. I -- "

"Are you still married?"

"No, you?"

"No, not for a long time." He smiled his sexy smile and placed a hand over mine. "I have a busy job that takes me all over. Do you travel with your job?"

"Yes. I regularly go to Scarborough and Whitby, and the other way to Leyburn and Darlington and Durham. Much further afield when I have to… all over really… I cover quite a large area."

"I go to all of those places. We'll have to meet up. Do you stay over anywhere?"

"Sometimes, when I have early or late calls," I said, aware of the tingling that his hand had set off in my arm. God, he was so attractive and I liked how he was looking at me.

"You are lovely, Laura, so attractive and I love your smile. I feel as if I know you already. Shall we have another?" he asked raising his empty glass. "And a bite to eat?"

Oh boy did I like this guy!

We spent over three hours together and he didn't smoke nor drink too much. He was ambitious and hardworking, and obviously liked me.

When he did get up to leave, he apologised saying he had a late call to make on the way back to Newcastle. He worked for a large car company and was manager of the on-going service division. He asked where I would be the following week.

"I have an early call in Kingston-Upon-Hull on Tuesday and as I will be in Selby and Goole on Monday. I'll stay there in Kingston and work my way back on Tuesday along the coast."

"What a coincidence I'll be there too next week, on Tuesday and Wednesday night. We must meet up for dinner. Where are you staying?"

"Usually The Holiday Inn or somewhere similar."

"City centre?"

"Yes, usually. You?"

"I'll book in there so that I can see you home," he said with a knee trembling smile.

Well, I thought, *that will make my journey worthwhile.* I was dreading going to Kingston upon Hull as it was difficult to park and find my way around, but now I would have the pleasure of seeing Ben for dinner and... who knows?

He was there, of course, looking as tempting and sexy as I remembered. We found a little French restaurant and had a lovely, flirty evening eating grilled fish with loads of garlic and spices, drinking too much wine and walking back to the hotel with our arms wrapped around each other. He set my whole body tingling and I couldn't have moved away from him even if I wanted to.

I was transfixed by his sexy smile, the way he touched me and leaned down toward my face as if he couldn't take his eyes off me. He made me feel there was no one else around and that we were in some sort of magic bubble.

I had never before been so attracted to anybody, and yet there was something... I couldn't put my finger on it. He was deliberately moving me into his space... I could *not* resist... I felt out of control and yet I went willingly to his room.

"Stay with me?" he said.

"Yes," I murmured. "I'll have a shower and bring my things to your room."

"Come back here," he insisted, "and you can shower while I make some business calls." So, I brought my case to his room and he was already on the phone making appointments for the next day or week and I could hear him demanding attention from who ever he spoke to.

I crept past him into the bathroom and immersed myself in the hot spray of the shower, wondering what on earth I was letting myself in for. I couldn't have ever imagined that I could be in a stranger's room, knowing so little about him, wanting him, completely and utterly beguiled by him so that I was prepared for whatever he offered.

Stepping out of the shower, I found Ben waiting with a towel, which he wrapped around me pinning my arms to my body. My wet hair trailed across my face and I laughed self-consciously as he rubbed my back. Without warning, he stepped backward, taking the towel with him. I tried to retrieve it but he threw it behind him and put up his hands.

"Stay still... Let me look at you."

"No, no." A deep blush spread, and I placed my arms across my chest.

"Will you stand still and put your arms down?" His tone was soft yet commanding and I found myself obeying, and feeling like a schoolgirl. Here I was in front of a virtual stranger, standing naked with dripping hair. I scraped my hair away from my face and watched his eyes looking at me. He scanned me from head to toe almost like he was inspecting an object, and I felt exposed and started to shiver.

"Why are you nervous?" he asked.

"Give me the towel... You're looking at me as if I was a racehorse or something." My voice was shaky. "It's -- "

"It's what?" he interrupted and stepped forward. "It's lovely, and you're lovely, beautiful and desirable, and I want you."

My resolve was melting by the second as he wrapped his arms around me. His long fingers trailed across my back and the sensation was like a warm caress of sunshine. I could feel the muscles in my back soften as his right hand stroked the curve at the base of my spine and the other swept upwards to hold the back of my head, his fingers in my tangled hair. He drew me towards him. I couldn't look up or turn my head as his grip tightened, and he pressed into the small of my back so that my body arched towards his, pulling me onto my tiptoes, my forehead rested on his warm, hard body. I could feel my pelvis open to greet the hard bulge in his trousers.

I'd never before felt so completely controlled. He took hold of the back of my hair and tilted my head backward so that our faces were close. His breath was hard and fast, and his lips were on my forehead, kissing where I had cut my head. He was so tall. I had to lean back to kiss him. Oh, how much I wanted to kiss him, to explore his mouth and face with my tongue. With quiet precision, his lips explored the soft contours of my ears and neck. My arms wrapped around him and our lips met.

We kissed sweetly at first but then with a fervent passion, as if we were never going to stop. His tongue filled and explored my mouth. Without taking his lips from mine, he leaned away and opened the zip and belt of his trousers. With the same hand, he pulled my arm and guided my hand to his hard, hot penis.

I suddenly felt the need to look at it. It was so much bigger than I'd expected. I pulled away from him and let my eyes drop to his amazing tool. I'd never had the desire to suck Brian's penis or my more recent lovers, even at the height of our pleasure, which was such a long time ago I can hardly recall. I do know that at that moment, I wanted to take it into my mouth and pleasure this gorgeous man. It surprised me, but I bent forward holding his penis and guiding it to my lips. I heard a slight moan as I opened my mouth over the hot tip and sucked. Oh, bloody hell, for a moment I felt so powerful and in charge. He moaned gently but as he pushed forward I felt panicky that he would force it too far into my mouth and when his hands started to push at the back of my head, I pulled away.

"Come on, come on, don't stop, suck me."

"Sorry," I gulped and drew away, my legs feeling weak. No, this wasn't what I wanted... and yet as he lifted me and pushed me down onto the bed, I wanted him.

His expression was dark and all trace of the sexy smile was gone. He looked hard and threatening, so my heart leapt as he stepped backwards out of his trousers. I started to object but my body was tingling and waiting, and the need to have him inside me was so intense. I had never felt anything like this before. Every cell in my body felt on edge and it absolutely took my breath away, desire for sex had never been like this for me.

He leaned over me, "You want me, don't you? Tell me you want me, beg me to fuck you."

"Yes, I do."

"Tell me, Laura, come on say it," he insisted, holding me with both arms pinned to the bed. He was looking into my eyes and I couldn't focus properly. It was as if he was looking into my thoughts, his expression hard and determined. "Come on, tell me what you want. I want to hear you say it. I'm going to let go of you and I want you to beg me to fuck you. Lie still... lie still I want to look at you."

Every word and his sardonic looks intensified my desire for him. Kneeling beside me, he bent over and put his lips on my belly and kissed and sucked me as if I was delicious ice cream, one hand caressed my breasts, and my nipples were hard and hot.

"Come on, Laura. Tell me what you want. Tell me. Say it out loud," he said again. His tongue trailed downward, he pushed my legs apart with one hand whilst the other squeezed and rolled my nipple until it hurt. The pain was exquisite and his fingers explored me. He moved between my legs, released my throbbing breast and bent forward and pushed his tongue into me. I moaned from deep inside myself. Just as my body wanted to explode, he leaned back and opened me with his thumbs. His eyes were dark and his mouth tight as he said, "OK, Tell me what you want, pretty lady." He was looking at me with intense passionate desire and I felt a wave of fear as I watched his hard body bearing down towards me.

"Fuck me please," I whispered, "please." I could hardly breathe never mind talk, but at the same time, I wanted to scream out loud with the sheer intensity, the sensational quivering that was happening inside me, wanting to be penetrated. He entered me faster than I would have liked and then immediately thrust with slow deliberate strokes so that I felt compelled to move my hips up to meet him. I can only say that I have never had such intense physical pleasure at the same time as being repelled by the man who was giving it to me. His lips were parted and his teeth clenched as he rode my body. All the while, his eyes were fixed to mine and I couldn't drag my focus away from him. It was like being hypnotised. Suddenly waves of sheer delight overtook me and I lifted my hands to his face whilst my body throbbed and sang with an exquisite soaring orgasm, the like of which I'd never before experienced.

It was over a week until I heard from Ben again and I'd left him at least three messages on his mobile, the only number I had for him. I wasn't going to ring again and found myself wondering what Teresa would advise. I was sure that she'd say walk on, don't let it get at you but I was letting it get to me. My rather fragile ego was taking a beating. As experienced as Teresa was, she believed strongly that that there were strict rules to the game. I was so dismally out of practice that I wasn't sure how to play hard to get. I guessed this was the time to play it cool. I had already proved to him how sexually emancipated I was by staying with him in his hotel and indulging in the most rampant sex that I had ever experienced.

I was in something with Ben, feeling things so deeply... but it wasn't love. I wasn't even sure whether I really liked him, but hell, I wanted him. He'd set all my nerve endings on edge, and I was constantly aware of the physical need I had to repeat our sexual romp. I glowed at the thought of it and found myself blushing, remembering how incredible it had been and anticipating the next time. When he called, I was breathless with excitement.

"How's it going?" he asked. "Before you ask, I've been over to Dublin on business and it was quite unexpected. I often have to go. We have a big distributer there. Are you OK?"

"I'm fine," I said as casually as I could. "Where are you off to next?"

"Let me ask *you* where you are going and I will fit my itinerary around that. I have more freedom than you do."

"I have a night in Scarborough this week, and next week an overnight in Leeds as I have to go to Head Office for some sort of update on the deals they're offering shops."

"Where are you staying? I think I need to see you again soon. I have something very special for you."

Oh boy, I just knew I had to see him again so we arranged the time and the place to meet up in Scarborough two days away.

The anticipation was intense.

***

CHAPTER 14

The sea air was invigorating and the weather was sunny and much milder. It was six o'clock when I rushed into the foyer of my hotel. I was flushed with excitement and anticipation. Ben was waiting for me in the bar and my heart nearly leapt out of my mouth. He downed the remains of his drink and stepped towards me. His heavy-lidded eyes and sexy smile had me bewitched, and as he took my hand and led me to the lift, I was already hot and ready for him. We kissed as we ascended and if we hadn't reached the fourth floor so quickly I would have given in there and then.

Once inside his room, we said nothing but devoured each other with our hands, lips and tongues. Never before had my body felt so out of control.

Before we had any sort of conversation, my jacket and blouse were off and he had me pinned up against the door, pushing his hot body into mine. He undid my bra so skilfully and bent his head to my breast, nibbling and teasing so that I could hardly breathe. I pulled at his clothes and with his jacket and shirt discarded he undid his trousers so that I could touch him. God, he was burning hot, and before I could take a breath, he had turned me and pushed me onto the bed face down and quickly and roughly yanked both my skirt and my panties down far enough to enter me from behind. His fingers opened me but I was already wet and he pushed into me easily while his fingers moved against my clitoris. We were both on our knees, and my face was buried in the floral bedspread.

We reached orgasm so quickly and then lay breathless beside each other, holding hands and surveying the untidy mess of clothes and shoes all over the room.

"Just for starters, darling," he said eventually.

The whole evening was beyond anything I had ever experienced before. For the main course, Ben made me wait so long for satisfaction that I was exhausted. He made me sit, lie down, then I had to stand, then beg him. He loved the idea that he was in control, and seemed to take pleasure in humiliating me. I was amused at first but then he pushed me onto my knees, squeezing my shoulders hard and made me ask him to fuck me, put his cock into my mouth and holding my head in his hands, pushed in and out slowly holding the back of my head by my hair and then he pulled out and lifted me up onto the bed, opened me roughly, pushing first his fingers and then his tongue into me until I felt like screaming.

"You're so wet. You want me, don't you, baby?"

"You're hurting me."

"I want you to be sore so that you don't forget the pleasure I give you."

With that dark, sadistic, sexy look, he sat back and stopped, demanding again that I begged him to come into me whilst holding me open and flicking my clitoris. My nerve endings were crying out, and eventually he pushed himself into me and holding my hips moved me up and down vigorously until I couldn't hold on any longer and crying out exploded into the most amazing orgasm. I called out his name and he groaned with satisfaction. Oh it felt so good... and yet I hated him for his power over me.

We only ate a meagre amount of the chicken and salad ordered from room service but drank at least two bottles of red wine and my body felt violated and weary by the time I finally fell asleep. He was not even comfortable to sleep with, his hard body turned away from me and when I reached out to touch him, he squirmed and moved us further apart.

I left early the next morning not even having checked into my own room. I would have to find an excuse to give to Miss G-G. My body was sore and my shoulders bruised and I didn't hear from him that week so I tried not to think about him but used my work as a distraction.

I had a call from Ed about the inquest and funeral. 'Accidental death' due to an overdose of various drugs, all illegal. I sent flowers and commiseration to his family. I thought about him a lot that day. How long ago that all seemed to me now.

I didn't hear from Ben the week after, but I couldn't even escape those dark, sardonic eyes in my dreams. I found myself waking in the night hot and delirious with need for him. I pushed myself through the training day in Leeds and hoped that everyone just thought I was a bit under the weather. I was definitely not my usual upbeat self. I couldn't think about him without some regret and dislike, but punished myself over and over for being so acquiescent, for allowing him to play me, but then my thoughts changed so that I hated myself for not being what he wanted, knowing that he was only toying with me, but then not caring. Every time the phone rang, I leapt at it, hoping to hear his voice. I wasn't eating properly either.

He did eventually call on Saturday, just as I came in from town with a pile of shopping. I was determined to be cool and relaxed with him but in less than a minute, he set my heart beating fast again as he convinced me that he had had to deal with an emergency delivery of parts that were coming from Japan and he had to fly out to oversee the order. My spirits lifted and I immediately felt pulled back into his spell.

His voice was slow and sexy as he said, "Can I see you soon? I've missed you so much."

133

"OK. Will you come here or shall I come to Newcastle?" I asked.

"No, I'm in Scotland at the moment and I have loads of calls this coming week. Tell me where you are and I will arrange my travel so that we can meet up."

"Can we eat and talk this time?"

"Of course, darling. It was all a bit frantic last time wasn't it?" he laughed. He was sweet and charming and before I knew it we had arranged our next meeting in a hotel in Penrith. I had a late call in Pooley Bridge on Monday and an early one in Brough on Tuesday.

This time we had dinner in the hotel restaurant, flirted, held hands and talked. He told me about his rather unusual upbringing; born in India with a series of Armahs. He never saw his mother who socialised all the time and drank heavily. His father was a strict Presbyterian minister who disapproved of everything, including his wife, Ben's mother. She died in rather unusual circumstances, but he didn't know anymore than that. Ben was only seven when he was sent to Scotland to boarding school and stayed there until he was thirteen when he went to live with an ageing uncle in Perthshire who had little time for him but was his only remaining relative. He saw his father only once before Ben left for University in Bristol, the furthest distance he could get away.

"No other family at all?"

He shook his head. "No, but I've had a good life, travelled a lot, even went back to India to see what I could find out about my mother. But I drew a blank."

I pictured him as a sad, disturbed little boy and understood his loneliness from not having a mother around. It made me wonder again about his life, his seeming isolation, lack of friends and his attitude to women. I asked him again if he was married.

"I've already told you that I am not… but I used to be a long time ago. It was short and definitely not sweet," he laughed, but his steely blue eyes were serious.

"Don't you trust me baby? I've been on my own a long time."

"How long?"

"Does it matter? You and I are good together. I want to see more of you. I'll try to get my schedule slowed down a bit and we can do some real life stuff like shopping and walking and cooking together." He made it all sound so normal and my heart leapt as he stroked my hand.

What was I doing? How was it that I had managed to get swept along on this great breaking wave that left me breathless? I felt desperate but at the same time wildly excited. I'd dismissed his sadistic, hard self and allowed myself to glow with delight as this handsome, charming man made our relationship sound like it was important and on-going.

"I'm so sorry if you think I don't care about you, but you must know that my job is very demanding and I do get carried away with what is going on."

"Just call me and tell me where you are and what you are doing," I said. "How hard is that?"

"I should, yes, I know, but I am just a bit thoughtless, I guess." He looked sexy and appealing as he smiled at me.

"I'll tell you now that I will be in Dublin for the next two or three weeks so don't worry, but I *will* call you… I promise… Let's go to bed now, baby."

His hand was caressing my thigh and I could feel myself responding to his touch. I needed to be cool and less responsive but I found myself wanting him but I made him wait while I got changed and brushed my teeth in my own room. This time, when I got to his room, he was gentler with me and I felt that our conversation had

135

really made a difference and that he was beginning to understand my needs. He still maintained control and wanted me to obey him but it was softer, more enjoyable that night. He left with a promise to see me again soon, certainly before going to Ireland.

We met three days later and I arrived late at the hotel. The sex was quick and hard and again, I felt his powerful control over me. We hardly talked except when he was telling me what to do and we devoured each other with a hungry passion as we had in Scarborough. He left at seven the following morning saying. "Soon, baby I will have more time."

I didn't want our relationship to be totally sexual but two weeks later with no contact, I felt so let down and worried again that I was sure now that he didn't really mean his clever seductive words. But again, when he called me, my resolve disappeared and he charmed me into another meeting. I was angry and told him that I didn't want it any more. Just meeting and fucking.

"Let's have a proper date then. Where would you like to go? What would you like to do? I'll take you anywhere you want to go. I promise I will make the time."

Trying to snatch back an atom of dignity from the situation, I said, "To the theatre or the cinema… anything normal so that--"

"Will I be able to keep my hands off you for so long? I don't think so."

He laughed but eventually agreed. It was to be closer to home this time and no hotel and we were going to go to the cinema and have dinner together, a proper date.

Then I got an unexpected call to be in Leeds again and… yes, he was there. How amazing that his calls could always be made to coincide with mine.

He was standing in the bar waiting for me when I got back to the hotel and I was overcome by his sheepish, sincerely apologetic smile.

"I've missed you so much," he said, taking my hand and sending shivers through my body. "We'll do the date another time, I promise." He lifted his hand to my face. "You want me, I can tell. Have you missed me, baby?" His slow sardonic smile revealed how pleased he was to be having such an effect on me. My body visibly shook as he stroked my cheek. I couldn't wait to feel his hard body next to mine. I hated myself for letting him do this to me yet again… I am confused… I did want him and the pleasure he gave me however painful or humiliating he made it. I hated myself for wanting it so much.

He took my clothes off slowly that evening and hardly touched my body at all. He made a point of *not* touching me but held my chin and pushed his tongue into my mouth. I lifted my arms to hold him close but he stepped back and hissed. "Stand still and wait. I want to look at you, my lovely lady."

My shameless need for Ben disturbed me and I seemed unable to have a rational thought. He stood back, looked at my naked body and I started to cry, my burning tears pouring silently down my cheeks. I can't explain why, I am usually such a strong person, but all my confidence seemed to have run dry. At that moment I would have done anything to bring him close to me.

"It's OK, baby… be still." He stepped toward me and swept his thumbs across my face. He looked into my eyes and smiled his sexy smile. "I'll give you what you want if you do as I tell you. When I tell you lie down open your legs wide and wait." He turned his back on me and started to take off his clothes.

"Stand still and wait," he ordered over his shoulder.

No, I won't. I'll leave, I thought. *You have no right to make me feel like this. You are enjoying seeing me upset and obedient.* I bent to pick up my clothes but he spun around and held me against the wall with his hands on my neck.

"Are you going somewhere? Not leaving me are you, lovely lady? I did tell you to stand still and wait." His grip tightened and he pressed his thumbs into my throat so that I could hardly breathe, my heart beating with fear. His eyes were hard and cold.

"Let go of me," I spluttered.

"There's no need to look so worried I won't hurt you… too much," he snarled in my face. He tipped my head back and holding my chin with one hand, he caressed my face and neck with the other. "Do as I ask, Laura" he said, then bent his head and bit me hard on the shoulder. I sobbed silently, hot tears running down my face but as his grip slackened for a moment, I pulled away from him but my back was against the wall and he stepped forward so that I couldn't move. He took hold of my nipples and started to rotate them with his thumb and forefinger squeezing harder and harder, so hard that I was now sobbing loudly, my face was distorted with fear. I didn't even resist. Looking into my eyes, he said, "These are so beautiful and they are all mine, aren't they Laura? Aren't they baby?" I couldn't move. He twisted a bit more. "Tell me when to stop," he said, smiling.

"Stop now please," I begged and he released me so very slowly that I held my breath in case he pinched hard again. Then he gently licked my reddened nipples and put his fingers inside me. Against my will and all common sense, I felt my body respond instantly and was ashamed of myself for being so weak and still wanting him so much. *Sadistic bastard.*

He took me fast and hard when he was ready and this time, I didn't want to respond and I didn't get to an orgasm. He then caressed and stroked me because I was still crying. I felt so weak. *This has to stop,* I thought.

I'm not usually a passive person and I have never been a victim of abuse, nor have I ever questioned my self-worth and yet, here I was behaving like fodder for a control freak. I definitely don't fall into the category of feeling that I don't deserve better and yet I let this happen. "Why do you want to hurt me?" I asked.

"Baby don't cry. I didn't really hurt you, did I? You know it's only because you drive me crazy and I want you so much." He smiled and kissed me softly, his hands caressing my hair and my face.

***

CHAPTER 15

I called in to see Teresa on my way back from work one day. She took one look at me, put the kettle on and said, "What's going on, hon? You look as if you need to offload something."

I'd lost weight and I knew I didn't look good.

"Oh, I'm just tired," I said, hesitating.

"I think you need to slow down and travel a bit less."

"No, it's not the traveling" I said and started to tell her about Ben and how he made me feel, and the incredible sex. I didn't tell her about the pain and the humiliation I felt and that I was becoming so needy and affected by it but I think she could see that. Her expression said it all. She knew me well enough to know there was something really wrong.

"Sounds a bit obsessive to me, hon. If it's affecting you like that, it really isn't good."

"I know." I felt my stomach clenching and tears came into my eyes, which I wiped quickly away. Teresa handed me a bunch of tissues and put a cup of strong coffee in front of me. I hated myself for not having more self-control.

"Sounds like he's married, if you ask me." Plonking herself on the chair opposite me she looked at me steadily, "Have you been to his place yet?"

"No... Do you really think he is married? He told me he wasn't and we only meet in hotels because he travels so much. I do believe him. Maybe it's because I want to but I think I would know, don't you?" I said sullenly, as I tried to control my shaking hands.

"Hell's teeth, Laura. Men are really good at deception, just be careful. Ask him again."

"I have and I've even had a look online to see if I could find him on the electoral register, but I can't. I'm not even sure that he has given me his real name. Oh hell, Teresa, this man has had a devastating effect on me and I'm not sure I like it. How could I have let him get under my skin?" Tears rolled down my cheeks again and Teresa put her arms around me.

"Get rid, hon. You don't need a guy like this in your life however much pleasure he is giving you."

"I feel like a stupid teenager but I don't even have that excuse anymore. And I don't want to make the same mistakes." I sniffed.

"He sounds like a game player to me. You definitely don't look healthy on it. Does he hurt you?"

"No," I lied.

The next week was busy and I had two calls near Newcastle so I called Joe to see if he was available. It was his birthday the next day and I had a couple of presents for him. He was doing well with his course in Agriculture and Environmental studies and was happy to let me treat him to lunch. He was going to be home very soon and would be staying for several weeks because he was going to be on work experience with a team of people locally creating a new Middlesbrough Urban Farming project planned from the end of October until January the following year.

I was finished for the day so we met just outside town, had a leisurely lunch together and off he went back to uni. I strolled along to where my car was parked and felt better for seeing Joe, even though he had commented on how tired I looked. I made up my mind to stop obsessing about Ben who clearly hadn't given me a thought in the past two weeks.

I turned the final corner and the cold wind swished at my hair and my coat. I stopped for a moment to look for my car keys and there he was, ahead of me; Ben in his long, dark cashmere coat and for a single second my body started to move toward him. I knew he had an address somewhere in Newcastle but he had never told me where. I wanted to approach him, but he wasn't alone and I stepped back aware of my heart beating in my chest, my breathing had stopped. What was he doing here? He was supposed to be in Dublin.

The woman who walked beside him with such an easy grace was dressed in a long camel coat and a colourful expensive scarf. The wind was blowing it up and she lifted a slim hand to retrieve it, holding it in place. She was tall and dark haired, not young, probably ten years older than me, but attractive. She had an air of confidence and elegance.

They weren't touching. Instead their body language spoke louder than words. Two people walked past them with a pushchair and she moved away from him but straight away stepped back close to him. He held out his arm, she smiled and leaned toward him. These were two people who knew each other well and were totally comfortable together. As they walked on, his left hand was resting protectively on the base of her spine and I could see quite clearly that he was wearing a wedding ring.

Of course he was married, it all made sense: no family or friends to meet, the absences, the lack of calls and the hotels. They stopped and turned together and entered a red brick house with steps to the front door through a small terraced garden. He took a key from his pocket and opened the door and she proceeded him in. At that moment a couple of children turned the corner and whooped by on roller skates and he turned, his eyes lifting to look at them.

I was standing so close I was sure that he would see me. He didn't but then he didn't expect to.

I watched spellbound. He wasn't far away but was unaware of me, or anybody else, or of being watched.

It's a funny thing, when you see someone you know and so unexpectedly and you know they haven't seen you, you get a fresh and different impression. I recognised how old he looked, more like fifty eight than forty eight, his dark sexiness seemed slightly grubby and he was shrugged into his coat against the wind so didn't look as tall as I remembered. His clothing was smart but I could only think of him naked beside me.

Had I suspected? Of course I had, but it didn't make the reality easier to bear. I was shaking and feeling sick. It was all wrong. How could I have been so stupid? Turning away and with trembling legs, I walked back to the car. A sharp wind was blowing and my now-long hair was flicking around my face as I tried to stop my shaking hands and unlock the car door. I sat for several minutes behind the wheel, trying to sort my thoughts and feelings. I felt humiliated and foolish but berated myself for not allowing myself to recognise the signs. They had all been there, the constant absences and the hotel meetings and never really ever meeting any of his friends or colleagues. I had also discovered with some dismay his immense capacity for secrecy. He would tell me only what he wanted me to know, perhaps that he was going away on a job, working late, attending a meeting, and that would be the end of it, more information as to his plans or destinations would not be forthcoming. He would never explain why he didn't contact me for days on end.

'OK, Laura pull yourself together*. In truth, in the short time I had known him, he had not exactly treated me well. Yes, he had fucked the socks off me, made me realise what a powerful sexual drive I had and taken me on a journey of delight and pain I never thought possible. But he also made me cry, humiliated and hurt me, never really taken me out, suggested a holiday or a day out together, never even let me take him home. Always a hotel room, in his time and at his beckoning.

Really is that what you truly want from a man? Hell, no, no... NO.

I revved the engine and decided that Benton Blaze was not going to play with me any longer. I would not even reproach him. I would just tell him that he was no longer part of my life and I would move on.

I drove back to my home, completed my orders and set my schedule for the next day before I resorted to drinking a couple of glasses of wine and ate two packets of crisps, and by the time I had showered and got into bed, I wanted nothing more than a good night's sleep but I lay tossing and turning before I could convince myself that he was not worth my time or my body, and I would not be humiliated by him again.

I don't even like him. I kept telling myself and I truly didn't. I certainly did not want to be involved with a married man, so I decided that I would discontinue my internet dating and concentrate on my family and friends.

I refused his phone calls and texts, replying only to his e-mail message asking me what was wrong. I'd replied, 'You told me you weren't married. I do not have relationships with married men.'

A huge bouquet of flowers arrived. 'With Love' it said on the card. He'll think that's all it takes to get me back into his bed. He knew what an incredible effect he had on me and how I longed for his touch, but having lied and cheated and hurt me, I was determined not to let my need for him take me down a pathway that I didn't want to go.

For several nights, I lay staring at the dark enclosed space of my bedroom. I craved sleep but despite the gnawing fatigue that overwhelmed me, I could not calm my thoughts. In the quiet of the night, small noises disturbed the heavy darkness. I took some deep, slow breaths as I had learned from doing yoga and then curled myself into the foetal position. I tried to shut out my persistent thoughts but still I couldn't sleep. Faintly in the distance, I could discern the gentle hooting of a night owl.

My whole world has changed, I thought, *all because my body desires a man I don't even like. How can I ever trust my own judgement again?* I'd willingly allowed myself to get into this situation. It's crazy and I dislike myself for being so confused. I had an incredible sense of loss but I couldn't understand why and that somehow made it worse. I'd always believed in equality and respect and never imagined that I could want someone who inflicted so much pain, both emotional and physical on me.

As the thin bleak light of dawn began to appear, the urgency of rest became absolute but I got up anyway, heavy-eyed and pale.

Joe was back home now for the next few months and I was so pleased to have him there. Several times he had asked, "What's up Mum?" and I could only reply, "I'm not sleeping well, that's all."

Stuart telephoned and asked me out, but I was too tired and listless I said, "Sorry, I couldn't possibly at the moment."

"Are you ill?" he enquired.

"No, just tired." I know I was abrupt.

"Is there anything I can do?"

I wasn't in the mood to explain and I'd become grumpy and bad company. "No, no you can't... thanks."

I got off the phone and started to cry. I was so ashamed of myself but I cried and cried. There are times when you think you'll cry forever but eventually the sheer exhaustion of it forces you to calm down and start breathing again. I drank a whole bottle of wine, then I hid from Joe that night, left him a note with the excuse of a migraine and went to bed before he came home. Flo came and sat on my chest and purred softly, licking the tears from my chin. Her unconditional love warmed my heart, but I lay in bed tossing and turning, crying into my pillow until it was soggy and myself exhausted.

It was November again, cold and bleak and that's how I felt. Christmas was looming and I was drinking rather more than usual and even stopped at a local wine bar on a couple of occasions and then drove home, something I would never normally do. I drank at home too and sometimes took a glass to bed with me hoping that it would help me sleep. Of course all that happened was that my thoughts became more confused and although falling asleep might have been easier, it didn't last long, and I would be awake again feeling nauseous and miserable.

One day after work I felt really low, so I stopped in at the bar. I called Teresa to come and meet me but she was out. By the time I'd drunk a couple of gin and tonics and two large wines the edge of my tetchy mood had softened but I wanted more as everything seemed less sharp and spiky with a bit of alcohol in me. After another three or four, I was unable to stand easily and I knew that I drank far too much and was in no state to drive home, so I'd decided to phone Joe to come and get me.

He arrived to find me slumped against the bar, my jacket on the floor and my handbag lying on the counter. He wasn't impressed at my dishevelled appearance, my slurring speech and inability to walk straight and we had the first row we'd had in years.

"The times you've lectured me about excessive drinking… You are a horrible warning rather than a good example!" he shouted at me as I stumbled up the stairs and just reached the bathroom as I vomited into the sink, half of it splattering down the front of my lovely red jacket.

Standing at the bathroom door, Joe said quietly, "I thought you were OK Mum, but you're definitely not and I'm bloody worried about you. You smell like a barman's dishcloth. Look at the state of you." He walked away disgusted.

I was so upset and appalled that Joe had seen me like that and that it had caused us to row, I even broke one of my own unbreakable laws and called in sick the next morning.

Who was that woman staring back at me from the mirror? I looked terrible, my skin looked blotchy and pale, my hair lank and greasy, my eyes had dark rings beneath them and my hands were shaking.

I decided it was time to get some help. That day, having retrieved my car, I went to the surgery and begged to see a doctor.

"You're lucky. A cancellation's just come in," said the steely-eyed receptionist who also informed me that in the future I had to make an appointment. I must have looked needy and desperate as she kept glancing at me as I waited. I could see my reflection in the shiny glass door and I did look awful.

I saw old Doctor Stafford who I knew and told him I was depressed and that I wasn't sleeping. I didn't tell him what had happened to me or about the excessive drinking, but he was kind and said, "It often happens when marriages fall apart especially after so many years. It takes time to adjust to being on your own. You might think that you are coping well by getting on with working and suchlike but deep down your body is not. You say you're not sleeping either?" he said, writing a prescription.

"No," was all I could say.

"Laura, a short term dose of an antidepressant is probably all you need," he said handing me the prescription. "Knowing you, I don't think you'll need them for too long. Don't look so worried," he said when he saw my horrified expression. "Everyone needs a prop at some time in their lives. Take these for six months or so and unless things get worse, I think you'll be able to balance yourself out, so to speak. If not, get back here to see me again."

The prescription was for Prozac and although I was against the whole idea of anti-depressants, I needed help. I started taking them straight-away as I knew it would take about three weeks for them to kick in but very soon I began to feel better, so was unsure whether it was the Prozac or the fact that my resolve had increased, and perhaps the memory of Ben was beginning to fade.

I reflected that it was at the same time last year that I had my lovely holiday in Tenerife and had felt so good and positive about life and the future. So much had happened since then, meeting Gordon and his unusual friends and the good times we spent at his cottage together in the spring, my accident at Easter time and meeting up with Stuart again. June with Nick and Paula and the trip to London. The lazy summer days full of laughter and good humour with Simon, then Gordon's untimely and sad death in September. Then meeting Ben who'd turned my world upside down. I was angry with him and with myself for allowing this to happen and to be affected by such an unworthy man. I told myself that I was well rid of him and had made up my mind that no way was anybody going to do that to me ever again. I didn't need that in my life and I'd be much more careful with my emotions from now on. I *was* sleeping better but still occasionally when I thought about him, my insides lurched and I remembered that incredible thrill I got from being with him but slowly I was letting go and beginning to heal.

As the month went on, I felt better even though I still had the occasional sleepless night. I wasn't drinking at all and had even started my Christmas shopping and fished out my decorations.

Joe watched me carefully and worried about me if I came home late or seemed upset. By persuading myself, and him that I was fine, I gradually became so.

***

CHAPTER 16

I was unsure about what to do for Christmas so when Teresa invited me and Joe to her Christmas Day celebrations, I was delighted. She had also invited Tally and Michael, who would be together for a while in England to finalise the sale of Tally's business, and then they were going back to Jersey to plan their Easter wedding.

"It might be the last opportunity for us to be all together for Christmas with Tally going to live in Jersey," Teresa said sadly. "So we must make the best of it."

Her mother Megan, Megan's younger sister Aunt Gracie were also coming. Vic was invited too, although Teresa had the feeling that his children would take precedence.

Harry was still away counting mosquitos or whatever, so it would be seven or eight for Christmas dinner and we were to spread the load, knowing how busy Teresa was and divide the preparation and cooking between us.

All of us had had a busy year so we were looking forward to spending time together. We decided that I would make the puddings and mince pies, Teresa would get the turkey and ham and Tally who was brilliant with vegetables would prepare them all and cook them at Teresa's, and the fellas would organise the beer, wine and liqueurs.

Presents were to be 'Secret Santas' and each of us had taken a name for whom we would buy a present. My gift was for Aunt Gracie so it was easy as I know she had a liking for English Lavender products. Joe had to buy for Tally of which he was thrilled and bought her long drop, silver earrings with tiny pearl studs.

Christmas morning, the weather was wet and windy, with a forecast of storms later. Preparations made and loaded with food, presents and beer, we set off to Teresa's house in Kirkby, picking up Aunt Gracie from her house near Cleveland Nurseries on the way. She was ready and waiting with a huge poinsettia that waved about in the blustery wind, and a basket of chocolate and nuts, and her 'Secret Santa'. She laughed as she got in the car.

"Oh, how lovely this is. Let me check now before we go. I've got my keys haven't I?" she said, holding them aloft and then shoving them in her enormous handbag. "I've got my slippers and I have got my present for Vic... Oh, I'm not supposed to tell anybody who I bought for am I? Silly me... Laura, you look lovely," she said, admiring my newly-cleaned scarlet jacket. "And look at you, Joe, sooo handsome."

Dressed in her best plaid skirt and a rather over large orange jacket, she chatted happily until we arrived at Teresa's, remarking on Joe's height as we got out of the car. Joe was suitably polite and helped her with her basket and presents.

Teresa's house was beautifully warm and decorated in green, gold and red, the Christmas tree and the smell of cooking making the seasonal feeling complete. There she was, wearing a reindeer sprigged apron over her low-cut red dress. Pink cheeked and flustered from the kitchen, she greeted us with hugs and kisses. Joe took our coats upstairs and Aunt Gracie rushed in to see Megan who'd been staying over the holidays. Teresa was happy to see me looking so much better, having got rid of Ben, she wrapped her arms around me.

"Got me worried there for a bit, hon," she said. "Been there myself so I know... the bastard. You look great. Are you over him?"

"Absolutely," I replied, holding myself steady and hoping that saying it would make it so. "I'm fine. Don't say anything in front of Joe, will you?"

"No, of course not. What about Stuart? Has he been round again?"

"No, I've given up on him," I laughed but didn't tell her that I turned him down just a few weeks before. "Does Tal want any help in the kitchen?"

"I think everything's under control. Get yourself a drink and go and keep the boys company. Mother will be driving them nuts by now."

Megan was in full flow, asking everyone who they were and where was her daughter and why didn't 'they' have more chairs in the house. She couldn't remember being there before and thought Joe was the window cleaner. Aunt Gracie was endlessly patient with her and got her a sherry and a comfortable seat, then noticing that she had her earrings on back to front, calmly and quickly pulled off the clips and turned them around.

"There we are." She smiled at Megan's irritated look, and said sadly, "She remembers me most times, but not today. Megan was always the bright one you know, Laura."

What could I say? It was such a sad condition but other than the Alzheimer's, Megan was fit and healthy and didn't look unhappy.

Vic arrived with an armful of wine and presents and said he would go and see his children in the afternoon instead so Teresa was delighted, and wrapped her arms around him.

"Right, you're in charge of the booze. Now go see that everyone has a drink."

"OK." He smiled and went into the kitchen. We could then hear Tally laughing and telling him to keep out of her way.

"You two are doing well. How long is it now?" I asked Teresa when he was out of earshot.

"About two years. It's great. He's a good bloke and I got a bit fed up with the dating site… Are you going back on?"

"Yes, I will," I laughed. "You know what they say about falling off a horse? You gotta get right back on."

"Just be more careful this time. I want you fully functional and fighting fit. We've got a wedding to go to at Easter."

Tally heard the remark as she came out of the kitchen with a bowl of roast potatoes and shouted, "Yippee!" She hummed, 'Here comes the bride' as she plonked the bowl on the table, and with a broad grin said, " Get your bums on seats now, my darlings. It's all ready." With a bit of shuffling we got everyone sat at the table and Michael and Tally dished up the food while Joe and I cleared away the dishes as they were spent.

The whole day was noisy and fun. Silly hats were worn by all and we overfilled ourselves with food and wine and then too many chocolates and nuts. We sang a few carols and pulled the remaining crackers. Megan was at her best, asking about long-gone family members and reckoning it was about time Teresa had some children as she must be nearly thirty now.

"I wish," muttered Teresa, who was about to reach her forty-fifth birthday in January.

We exchanged presents and I got a pair of black leather gloves that I think Vic had bought.

Later after the Queen's speech, Tally and Michael snoozed, snuggled up together on the sofa. Aunt Gracie fell asleep on an armchair, mouth gaping and exuding loud snorts. Suddenly her false teeth popped out over her lips but she slept on. We couldn't stop laughing and both Tally and Michael opened their eyes and giggled with us. Megan saw the amusing side too but was still not sure who Gracie was.

Vic took off to see his family and Joe decided it was time to go mix with his own age group so called his best mate Craig, who lived nearby, to come and get him. Off they went, promising to be back before I left in the evening, but not before Joe said quietly. "You won't drink any more, will you Mum?"

Teresa was worried about Megan but she seemed happy in her own little world and later on in the day, she was quite lucid and chatted merrily to Gracie about Christmases when they were children. I could see Gracie laughing and smiling with her, happy that Megan had finally recognised her. It obviously hurt her very much to see her beloved older sister deteriorating so.

An altogether lovely day and Joe had come back to Teresa's quite tipsy and hugged me tight saying, "Mum, you're a star," and to Aunt Gracie, "We'll get you home safe, don't you worry, Aunty Grace," indicating the storm that had blown up outside.

"Say good night and get in the car, you great lummox," I said, knowing that he would sleep like a baby and wake with a thick head. Still, we had no plans for Boxing Day so we could both have a lazy day.

Christmas over and I felt good. Yes, I had enjoyed a few glasses of wine on Christmas Day, but I no longer had the need to dampen my feelings with alcohol. I wasn't even bothered about being alone New Year and suggested to Joe that he went out and enjoyed himself with his mates, and I would collect him and be his taxi for the night. He was delighted and went off to a party in Hutton Rudby while I watched the world celebrate on TV and had a glass of wine at midnight. I knew I had so many things to look forward to and that I was not remotely unhappy.

I collected Joe at one a.m. and before going to bed, we toasted in the New Year with a large brandy and coffee. He'd filled out in the last few weeks doing more manual work on the project and as he hugged me goodnight, I realised how grown up he was now, even though I still thought of him as my baby.

"Happy New Year, Mum," he said as he hugged me tight, "I'm glad that you're so much better."

"So am I, Joe," I said as tears filled my eyes and love for him filled my heart.

He was off again in a week or so to university and I would miss having him around.

January is a depressing month but I decided on a few new affirmations and a different attitude to my social life. I'd go back to my yoga class and try to structure my week so that I was home every Thursday so that I could attend. I found an application form for a painting class close by in Coulby Newham, filled it in and sent it off.

This year, my resolutions were also totally different:

Love

Grow some vegetables

Love

Cook more vegetables

Love

New car

Love

Get trim for Tally's wedding at Easter

Love

No sex without love

The weather was terrible, biting cold wind and sleeting snow showers. Business was slow. Nobody wanted to make appointments so I spent a few days contacting friends and family to wish them a Happy New Year.

Nick was worried when he told me that Paula would be having her surgery at the end of January. After that, more tests. They had decided to try to be positive about it and they'd also discussed adoption if they weren't able to have children. Nick didn't tell me any more but said he would call me soon with news.

"But regardless, we have set a date for the wedding, Mum. July 28th and we will be having it at Paula's parents... couldn't be happier. Will give you details soon."

"As long as you're happy, Nick. I will be too. Happy, happy New Year darling. Love to you both."

Maria's news was positive and she asked when I would visit again.

"When I win the lottery, my friend," I laughed, "but soon I hope."

Dad's blood pressure was causing him problems and he was off to the doctor's again. I told him I would visit the next time I was in Leeds.

I telephoned Ed too who was still very upset about Gordon and we talked for half an hour about him and his regrets about his own life.

Simon had been to Barcelona for Christmas with a new lady friend and told me that this coming year he intended to 'get off his bum' and do some real work.

I laughed and said, "About time too. Good luck and Happy New Year, Simon."

Tally and Michael were excited about their wedding at Easter and everything was booked, the invitations would be in the post soon, they told me.

"Get your flights sorted too, Joe, and we'll arrange accommodation for everyone," said Tally.

I would book our flight with Teresa and Vic so that we could all travel together. I had a good feeling about the coming year with so many happy events to look forward to.

***

CHAPTER 17

I decided it was time that I looked at the dating site again. I wasn't sure whether I wanted to use it anymore but with my new resolve, I felt I would be a bit more wary. There were nineteen messages, most of which I deleted immediately. How can someone in Devon or the Shetlands think they can form a relationship with someone in North Yorkshire.

Get real fellas, distance *is* an object when you're working or have a family or perhaps can't afford to travel.

Two messages caught my eye:

1. Antonio, 30 Aries from Darlington, 5'10"

Hello Lolly. What an attractive lady you are. Please come and meet me. I'm Tony, not brilliantly handsome but I brush up well and like to look after a lady.

Antonio. You are far too young.

Alan Pearson, 54 from Peterlee 6'2".

I am a good, kind man who has recently lost his wife. I am finding being on my own lonely and boring. You look like a nice, kind lady and I like your profile very much.

Possibly too old but will message him anyway. So I sent the usual, 'Hello, Alan. Would you like to chat on the telephone. Give me your number and I'll call you.'

The next day he messaged his number so I gave him a call. Within a few minutes, I knew that he was looking for a replacement for his dead wife as he told me all her wonderful characteristics, how well she cooked and kept the house spotless and that the person he was looking for must be a home lover who does not want to work.

"Sorry, Alan I love my job and wouldn't want to be at home all day but good luck in your search," I'd said.

A couple of days went by and I'd had no response to the two messages I had sent to John in Thirsk and Frederick in Durham so I decided to look at Antonio's again. I read his profile:

I am looking for an older lady for a tender, loving relationship, nothing too serious. I am a good bloke and have great respect for females. I think I know what pleases and I always put the toilet seat down.

Funny and nice, but still too young for me as I would be forty-three in the coming year. Then he had sent another message. *'Lolly, reply I am waiting for you.'*

'No, thanks. You are far too young for me.'

'What have you got against a younger guy?'

'Nothing at all. You are just too young.'

Then another.

'I could be just what you are looking for.'

'Antonio, go away,' I had replied.

Persistent this one. Another message.

'No, I want to meet you.'

'I'm too old for you.'

'No, you are not, you're absolutely perfect.'

'OK, just for coffee then.'

'It's a start. Can you come to Darlington?'

'Next Tuesday. The Bistro, Grange Street. eleven a.m. Coffee only.'

'Lovely, I will carry a red rose, see you there.'

'OK.'

So I met Tony who was like a breath of fresh air, open and honest and good-looking. He looked about the same age as Nick but he was just thirty and appealingly sweet natured. I felt like a 'cradle snatcher' but I liked him immensely and warmed to his immature sexiness. Nothing hidden or threatening, and I arranged to meet him again for a meal the following evening. He was blatantly sexy in his manner and his conversation. He made me happily aware that he was adventurous and needed a more mature lady to indulge his rather interesting fantasies.

"Nothing painful or cruel?" I inquired. I wasn't taking any chances again.

"What do you take me for?" he laughed "Oh no, just fun. Do you like chocolate ice cream?"

"Yes, I do."

"Well, let me get some and I'll spread it on my body so that you lick me all over. I like the sensation of cold ice cream and a hot tongue," he laughed at my surprised expression, "I'll do it for you too."

"I like champagne better."

"Champagne it is then."

I couldn't help but laugh as he told me that he liked a shaved pussy to match his own hairless state. Smooth and hairless was what he was, and what he liked.

159

"What completely?" I stuttered.

"Everything. I get waxed regular, smooth all over me. It's all the rage now. Want to find out?"

Tony was recently separated from his wife and had an eighteen-month-old daughter Rosie who he saw regularly. He wasn't looking for another wife and he just wanted some honest fun. He had an odd sort of charm but I no longer viewed charm as a quality in a man but I enjoyed my evening with him. He was tactile and flirty, so I was quite happy to go to his rather small bijou flat and we ended up kissing and caressing each other. He pressed his mouth into my cleavage until I assured him that he could go further. I had no illusions about my own need for a good fucking so I broke my new year's resolution and felt quietly ashamed that I was prepared to make use of this young sexy guy. He slipped his hands under my sweater and lifted it off in an easy movement. His shirt next, and then my bra. He rubbed his bare chest against my breasts. His body was smooth and young and yes, completely hairless. I was reticent about being naked in front of him but he stroked my body and as we discarded our clothes he told me that I was lovely, my skin so soft, my lips so kissable, he held my buttocks and grinned.

"I like you, Mrs Goddard. Do you like me too?"

"Yes, I like you too, young Antonio. You are so smooth." I grinned.

"What do you think about having a 'toy boy' then?"

"I'll let you know."

I could feel my confidence returning as this young good-looking, gentle guy kissed and caressed me. We made love and it was enthusiastic and athletic, but extremely pleasurable and completely uncomplicated, and afterwards, Tony brought steaming coffee and shortbread biscuits to the bedroom which we had sitting on his crumpled bed.

"Will I see you again?"

160

"Why not? That was fun."

"OK, next week, same time?"

"OK," I said, knowing I had a wide grin on my face.

So for the next four or five weeks, we repeated the fun and games. In between, we went to the park and played in the snow, drank steaming hot chocolate in the town, shopped for sexy knickers and bought an interesting unisex vibrator. In bed he played with me, teased me, turned me, twisted me, shaved me and I loved every minute of it. I found myself half-surprised and half-delighted that I enjoyed everything we did together so much.

"Let's try every position in the Karma Sutra," he giggled.

"You have to be joking... have you seen them. Everything has to bend every which way and I'm not standing on my head with my feet behind my neck for anyone," I laughed.

"All right but come here, I have an idea... just turn so... and then... " He moved one way and another so that we could try something different. He liked to give me a massage and was extremely good at it, a pleasure that I had not experienced before. I learnt a little too and he enjoyed being pampered. I thought at some point I might learn to do it properly. I was so totally unselfconscious with him.

We spread each other with chocolate, then champagne and made a terrible mess of his sheets. One night we sat in the bath with mountains of bubble bath and just played and massaged each other with baby oil when we got out. I looked forward to our meetings and knew exactly what they entailed. He was gentle and kind, a man of pleasure and fun. I didn't feel threatened or worried by Tony in any way.

We rarely drank any alcohol so it was sheer enthusiasm that heightened our pleasure in each other. This was healing for me and my spirit felt renewed and strengthened. So much of me had been

161

destroyed by my obsessive need for Ben. I was now enjoying sex with a man I liked. One night he asked me to tie him to the bedpost and blindfold him. He wanted to be teased. He wanted me to do something I had never done before. I looked nonplussed.

"Use your imagination," he said mischievously. I tied him and blindfolded him desperately trying to think of something different. I swished my hair around his smooth shaven equipment, I licked and nibbled him, trying to decide what I could do that he would like. Looking around for inspiration, I had a thought and reached to my iced water at the side of the bed and lifted out a large piece of ice.

"Open your legs," I said, and holding up his silky, smooth balls, I swiftly pushed the ice cube into his bum. He shrieked and laughed so much, I had tears rolling down my cheeks. I untied him and we fucked each other, laughing and squealing.

We had so much fun together but we also had a good relationship away from the bedroom. We talked about our lives and he told me what a strain he'd found it was on his marriage having a baby and how his wife didn't want him and all the usual things that happen as couples adjust to the demands of a third person in their relationship. I told him how normal that was and how having a child tests a relationship and teaches us to be selfless. He listened and asked me how I had felt and I told him about the stress and loneliness of not being able to feed Nick when he was born, how I'd felt such a failure because he didn't gain weight as he should. I was so young and every time the health visitor tut-tutted, I felt I was useless as a mother. I tried to explain about the tiredness and the changes that take place in a woman's body when she has a child and that strange feeling one gets of overwhelming responsibility for this tiny thing that has taken over your life. Anything else feels like an intrusion.

"Sex is the last thing on your mind when you have just given birth and it does require a bit of patience from the husband," I said.

"She didn't want to make love to me at all, not at all... Is that normal? We had such a good sex life right up until Rosie was born and after, just endless rows. She said I was selfish but I really tried to help as much as I could, but it didn't help at all. I thought she didn't care about me anymore and my needs were ignored. She constantly screamed at me. 'The baby has to come first.'" He said this looking like a sad lost little boy. I could see then that he was still in love with her.

"That's true," I'd said. "You can't ignore a child."

"I know that of course, but Rosie was a year old when I left and she wouldn't let me near her."

"I bet you hassled her," I said softly. "You didn't wait until she was ready."

"I guess I did," he admitted.

***

CHAPTER 18

So here I am in Tony's bedroom observing my satisfied smile in his mirror. I can only say that I now understand what Tally had been doing with Mark. Total commitment-free sex. It feels good, no pretences, no lies and no worries.

Of course it must end soon I know but I have learned such a lot. Sex and love are not the same thing and sex without love can be good or bad. Love without sex leads to trouble and although I'm sure there are many people who get over that, it is such a basic need, especially when you are young. Both together means commitment and honesty, absolute faith and a lot of laughter. After all, the sex act is probably the funniest thing most people do in their lives. Without the laughter and understanding, love can die and sex become a chore.

This is the last time we'll meet. Tony has told me that he wants to get back with his wife and being with me has helped him understand her better. He now feels that he can appreciate her feelings more than he did before and understands why she responded the way she did and he can now tell her how he felt when Rosie was born, without being angry or resentful. I'm so pleased and I tell him that I'm delighted to have known him and how he has helped and healed me too, given me back my confidence and brought me to an understanding of what I want and need from a relationship.

For the next month I concentrate on work and seeing Joe, and feel I know myself a little bit better. I'll still have few qualms about getting into another relationship, but I am done with playing. From now on I will not have sex with anybody just for fun or for lust but will wait for the right person, someone who I truly love and want. I really feel the last year had taught me about myself. What was wholesome and what was destructive, and particularly what was real and what was not.

Nevertheless, I do wonder sometimes whether I will ever have the energy to start a new relationship. The whole process of meeting that special person is so difficult as I've found from my internet dating. So many lonely people looking for love and that one special person and the chances of finding both love and desire and the 'glue' that Luis told me of seems so unlikely.

The weather is freezing and I'm having problems with my car, the heater has now packed up altogether and starting it in the cold weather is becoming very hit or miss. I decide I really do need to update my old Ford as it's now over ten years old and has done too many miles in the past twelve months. Definitely need some advice though: Joe is back in Newcastle, Vic on a skiing holiday at the moment and I have no idea what to buy or about models, horsepower and such like.

I decide that I will ask Stuart. He seems to know plenty about different engines, makes, models and so forth. I'd heard him talking to Joe about things like that last year. I found his card and noticed for the first time that he only lives a few streets away.

I call his number but there's no answer so I leave a message.

He calls back that same evening and says he would be delighted to help me. It's his week off so he has plenty of time.

When he arrives the next morning, I realise how long it is since I have seen him and am again overcome by his lovely eyes and sweet nature.

I wonder why he hasn't ever asked me out again, I think, *I must ask him,* so I say casually, "Stuart, do you remember when we first met? You asked me out and you have only ever tried once more and I was having a bad time and you have never asked me since. Can I ask you why?"

"No, I haven't, have I? I guess I thought that you wouldn't be interested."

"Why ever would you think that?" I'm so surprised that he hasn't picked up any of the signs of how much I like him.

"You were busy with all your dates. I didn't think you'd be interested in a boring old paramedic like me. Diane told me that you were always busy dating… 'all over the place' she said, 'out all the time.'"

"Diane my neighbour… How come she told you?"

"She told me the day I phoned for your number. 'You'll be lucky to catch her in,' she said, 'out all the time with her internet blokes,' and I thought that you must be having a really good time and then when I finally did pluck up the courage to ask you out, you were a 'stroppy mare' to me." He pushes out his lower lip in an exaggerated pout.

"Stroppy mare?" I giggle.

He smiles. "You were, you know."

"Oh, Stuart come here and give me a hug. You make me laugh so much and I should be furious with you for listening to my jealous embittered neighbour. I'll have to have words with her. I've always liked you and what's wrong with being a paramedic. You rescued me, didn't you?"

He wraps his arms around me and hugs me, then stands back and gazes into my eyes, his expression changing and before I can say another word, he kisses me soundly. "I have been waiting to do that since the moment I laid eyes on you," he says, "Come here, my love." This time he kisses me so tenderly and sweetly that I forget about everything, forgive Diane, and let myself melt into his arms, knowing instantly that my feelings are growing by the minute.

"Will you please ask me out now?" I say as I pull away from him. "I've been waiting so long. I really thought you'd gone off me."

166

"I did a bit," he jokes. "You don't make it easy for a simple Joe like me and I am incredibly jealous, so be warned. *Will* you come out with me, *please*? Where do you want to go and what do you want to do? Where do you want to live?"

"Hold on...What exactly are you suggesting?"

"Full commitment, the works, actually."

"I'm not sure I am ready for that yet. I have had a confusing year and I am still a bit unsure of myself. At the moment I am not even sure I want a full on relationship and -- "

"I'll wait as long as necessary but I know where I want this to go."

He is serious. I think to myself. "Steady now, we haven't even had a proper date yet."

"OK. We will start today, find you a new car first and then tonight we will have our first proper date and go out to dinner," he grins and says, "OK, let's go."

So here we are in the garage trying to decide what I can afford and what will be the most practical one for me. Stuart asks all the right questions and after much consideration, a test drive and a bit of haggling, we decide on a smart red VW Golf, good condition and low mileage. It'll be ready at the weekend.

We go to dinner in a little Italian restaurant that smells of basil, garlic and cheese and has a romantic atmosphere with candlelight and small intimate tables.

We order Spaghetti Bolognese and Stuart wants to re-enact the scene from 'The Lady and the Tramp' where they have a length of spaghetti and as they eat it they end up kissing. He makes me laugh as our lips meet and we make a mess on the tablecloth and the fat Italian waiter mops up a blob of sauce with an amused sigh while we giggle together. He has obviously seen it all before. As we drink our coffee, Stuart looks serious as he takes my hand in his.

"Laura, I can't tell you how much this means to me… being here with you. I've thought about it for so long now, I was beginning to have my doubts that it would ever happen."

"Well," I say lightly, "It just goes to show how bad I am at flirting. I thought I was giving you all the right signals, especially the day you brought me the vegetables and I tried really hard that day in Stokesley."

"I know. I thought afterwards that you were very 'friendly' that day but I just didn't have the nerve to ask and you were so busy."

Getting home I need to tell him how great the day has been.

"I've had a lovely time, Stuart," I say and the look in his eyes tells me he feels the same.

"See you tomorrow?"

"I'm going to Leeds tomorrow and popping in to see Dad after work," I explain.

"OK, I'll come round and bring you cocoa." He leans over and kisses me.

"Night, Stuart." I wave him off and go to bed with a warm glow and look forward to seeing him again.

I didn't, of course take him seriously but lo and behold there he is the next night outside my door holding a thermos flask. It is cold and ten o'clock. I burst into fits of laughter, "I guess you'd better come in then."

"I was hoping you'd say that. I'm freezing my bollocks off out here."

How good can someone make you feel? Cocoa and kisses and then to bed alone. He left knowing that I'd had a long day and was tired.

Today we are both free so we decide to go to York to see 'Pippin', a new show at the Joseph Rowntree theatre. We have a good lunch out and being together feels comfortable and normal as if we have known each other forever.

As another day draws to a close, we have a light supper and talk about our plans. I feel I can really tell him anything and he listens carefully and is not judgemental or smart.

When he kisses me, it is with such sweet simplicity and he holds me as if I am his most treasured possession. Yes, I'm enjoying the kisses but at the moment there is no stirring of sexual need or desire. I hold myself steady, feeling the closeness of this lovely man but I'm not going to let myself get carried away too easily. My physical reaction has slowed down with my new intent. I think I've shut down for a while and am pleased that I can go slowly and not just let my body decide. I'm sure that the time will come when I will want to respond on another level but it will be when I'm ready. I decide what I am experiencing at this moment is delightful and making me feel good in a totally different way.

At the weekend, I say goodbye to my old Ford and we pick up my new car. Stuart laughs at me when I say it matches my jacket, but I'm thrilled with it. We drive to Harrogate and have lunch, and do some shopping. I find a beautiful cream hat, huge, with floating rose petals all over the brim, and we both love it so I buy it for Tally and Michael's wedding. So now I need an outfit to go with it and some shoes. It's fun shopping with Stuart as he has a good eye for shapes and colours and he tells me that he would have liked to have been a designer but never quite got the right grades. We search the shops and eventually Stuart picks out the most perfect dress in rosy pink and cream, it fits and hugs my curves perfectly. I guess that the shoes will have to wait for another day as I have spent far more than I should have.

"I'll get you some," says Stuart.

"No."

"I know I'm only a humble paramedic but I can afford to treat you."

"That's not the point. This is only our third date."

"There will be many more."

"No doubt, but in the meantime I can buy my own shoes."

"When's your birthday?"

"Summer."

"I didn't get you a Christmas present."

"No, we weren't together then. Now will you stop arguing and let's get home?"

"Are we together now?"

I ignore him.

"OK, bossy boots."

He laughs at me as I wrestle with the enormous hat box. It's so huge we struggle to get it into the car. We stop for a drink on the way home and Stuart is thoughtful. He says seriously, "I need to ask you something, but it's a secret."

"Whisper so no one else can hear," I answer.

"Do you really want to know?" he says teasingly.

"I do really, is it important?"

"OK," he says and continues in a tiny voice getting softer and softer so I can't hear a word.

"What!" I raise my voice and the people on the next table turn.

With a smile and a wink he says. "Can we go home and play doctors and nurses?"

To which I reply, "Oh, you are so ridiculous. I haven't got time to play your silly games."

"Stroppy mare."

"Ha ha."

Such silly, amusing nonsense things that make me laugh. I am truly happy in his company and regret that we didn't get together sooner. But then I think, I wasn't the person I am now and I'm much more well adjusted than I was a year ago. All my experiences, good and bad, have brought me to a better understanding, not just of myself but also of the complications of relationships that I hadn't experienced before.

***

CHAPTER 19

Stuart unloads the car and I go up to my bedroom to take off my heels. He follows me up, shouting, "I'm bringing up your dress and the mighty hat box. Where do you want them?"

"In the spare room, please," I say as I hunt for my flat pumps, which seem to have crept under the bed. Bent over, I don't see him come into my room behind me.

"Can I see where you sleep? I imagine it, but want to see it."

I turn and smile at him but do not encourage him and drop my eyes.

"Does it make you nervous having me in your bedroom?" He steps toward the door as if to demonstrate that he didn't want me to feel that he was violating my territory.

"Yes, it makes me incredibly nervous. I've never had another man beside Brian in this room. That doesn't mean I haven't... you know... in fact I've been exploring myself... since he left... well, trying to find out what's it all about. I have to be honest with you." My words tumble out in disorderly confusion. "I've had five lovers since Brian left... all different... but I've never had any of them in here. It seems much more intimate somehow."

"Have you discovered what it's all about?" he asks looking concerned.

"No, not really. I'm not as confused as I was and I've had an amazing year, some good, some bad but I feel I understand my real needs so much better than I did."

"That's good isn't it?"

"It's the love thing. I don't know... It's all very confusing. I feel a bit drained and I am still not sure. I want to be sure."

"Ok let's put this on hold until you're more sure, Yes?"

"Yes, please."

Pulling on my pumps, I march to the door, turning so that I can get past him. Stuart doesn't let me slide past him but pulls me close and gives me a long hard reassuring kiss. Then we kiss softly and slowly, gentle tender kisses where our tongues explore and caress.

"Jezebel," he whispers in my ear.

"Not anymore. I've gone off the whole casual sex thing," I reply as we pull apart.

"It wouldn't be casual sex. If you have casual sex, when it's all over there's usually nowhere to go, and often you just want to get away. It wouldn't be like that for us, we have so much more. I want the time to be right for you though."

"I know."

"You have cold hands." He wraps his warm ones around my fingers and I lay my head on his shoulder.

I know that I'm not ready. Stuart sensing my feelings, smiles and moves away. "Come, my love, let's eat," he says as he leads me down the stairs.

Here's a man who knows exactly what I need at this point in my life. He makes me laugh all the time. His rather silly jokes and odd ways are charming and endearing. He never pushes me into any intimacy that I'm not completely comfortable with and only shows his affection when we are alone together. As time is moving on, our relationship thrives and we are getting closer and closer. Could I be falling in love?

Another new week and I have local calls and Stuart is on an early shift, so we meet at his house in the late afternoon. It's a large bungalow, detached with a big garden, greenhouse and shed. He's proud of his garden and insists on giving me a tour even though the ground's hard with the frozen remains of the overnight snow and there is little to see at this time of year. All the trees and shrubs are rigid with frost and the sky is dull and grey. It's really cold outside but his house is comfortable and homely inside with soft peach and coffee decor and dark, solid furniture. I notice everywhere there are photographs of a pretty blonde and a little girl.

I will let him tell me in his own good time, I think.

He has a huge wood-burning stove and when he has piled it high and it's burning brightly, we sit comfortably together and Stuart opens a bottle of wine then we toast each other and talk about our day. He's had a particularly harrowing morning dealing with a car crash on the A66, whereas my morning was dull and unsuccessful, as I have made no sales today.

His eyes wander once or twice to the photographs and his expression changes.

"I need to tell you about them," he says, indicating the photographs. His face creases and his eyes fill with tears. I take his hand and it's trembling slightly as he says, "It's hard to talk about, but you need to know and I know I need to talk about it too. They, my wife and little girl, went to a family reunion with relatives in Aberdeen nearly five years ago. I couldn't go because of my shifts and the crew was short-staffed. There had been a serious outbreak of flu and half the station was off sick." His voice is low and halting as he tells me about the fire. There were no survivors. His wife Anne, his two-year-old daughter Helena, Anne's aunt, uncle and her father all died together on that fateful day. Anne was only thirty-two and apparently they were all asleep when an old gas boiler exploded. Stuart had been told they would have died instantly.

I'm overcome with grief for him. I hold him to my heart and let him cry on my shoulder, tears running down my cheeks. I'm so pleased that he has finally let it out and we talk for an hour about his love for his family and how he's survived. His best friend also died in the past year from a rare form of cancer and he says it's made him realise that every bit of life must be lived and enjoyed to the full.

174

Although the whole evening is tinged with sadness, Stuart tells me he has learned to look forward not backward, and will not let the past haunt him. He's still trembling as he tells me that from the moment he set eyes on me, he felt a connection and was sure that our paths would cross again somehow.

"And they did," he says, forcing a smile. "That day I saw you on the pavement in Darlington with blood running down your face I felt as if the Gods were on my side… I was determined to look after you and get to know you and then when Diane told me about your internet dating I was devastated and -- "

"We're together now, that's all in the past." I interrupt him.

"Thank you. I feel so blessed," he says, kissing me lightly on the top of my head. Then with a smile, he leaps up and away into the kitchen to cook our supper while I repair my make up and know that I too feel very blessed.

I feel no jealousy or competitiveness with Anne, just an incredibly sadness and pity for what Stuart has had to bear, but I vow that whatever happens between us there would always be room for Anne and Helena.

Today, I discover that he is also an excellent cook and our meal of stuffed chicken breast with a lemon sauce, golden roast potatoes and spicy cabbage, all made from scratch, and is absolutely delicious. What talents this man has. Brian never cooked a meal in our entire marriage.

Walking me home, he holds me close and I know that he is relieved to have told me about his loss. He kisses me goodnight with the remark, "Do I have to go home with this swelling crotch?" and I laugh out loud at his amazing humour. "Tell me when you are ready, for God's sake, Laura."

"I will."

Another evening, Teresa arrives just after we finish eating and is somewhat taken aback to see Stuart in my kitchen, perfectly at home washing the dishes.

"So," she says, when I introduce him, "We meet at last. OK, what's going on? You look sooo happy both of you."

"Yes, we are," I say. Stuart grins from ear to ear. "He did finally get around to asking me out, with a little prompt," I added "and, yes, we are seeing each other. I take Stuart's hand. "We are doing OK thanks."

"Bloody 'ell hon. Am I pleased." She hugged me then Stuart and said, "Both my best mates fixed up. Let's phone Tal and tell her and get out the champagne. I feel like celebrating."

"Got some Cava. Will that do?"

While Stuart is pouring the drinks we phone Tally and tell her that Stuart and I have finally got together. She squeals her delight down the phone and promises to send him an invitation to her wedding straight away. He's so thrilled to be included, he slops the wine and we laugh and giggle as we mop up the mess and then lovingly toast each other.

Joe is home for the weekend, and is also pleased to discover that we are seeing each other. He liked Stuart from the start and I think he is secretly delighted that he doesn't have to keep such a keen eye on me. He admires my new car with Stuart and tootles off in it to see Craig. He's off back to Newcastle on Monday morning but he's really pleased to see me so happy and informs me that he's thinking of going skiing at half term. I remind him about Tally and Michael's wedding and that we'll be going to Jersey at Easter. "Can't do everything my darling. Plenty of time for skiing."

"Yeah, right. Wouldn't miss that," he says as he leaves.

***

CHAPTER 20

On the day that I know I'm ready to move forward with our relationship, I arrive at his house after I've had a particularly exhausting day. Although I am tired, I have hurried to see him again. I get a warm, tender sensation just thinking about him. I dream about him, I want to make him happy and I wake every morning with the knowledge of my growing love for him.

How pleased I am, I think to myself, *that he was in that garden centre that day.*

His eyes light up when I arrive. He relieves me of my coat and bags, takes my hand and sits me down to a beautifully set table in his dining room. He's taken such care with the simple setting, two purple candles adorn the table and the napkins are purple and white check. A single white rose sits in a cut glass container. Ella Fitzgerald purrs away in the background singing a soft, romantic song. On the sideboard there is a picture of his wife and daughter.

I know he's sincere and honest and that his feelings for me are genuine and caring as he says, "You do look tired, Laura. Are doing too much? This company that you are working for has given you a huge area to cover. How many miles have you done this week?"

"Don't worry so much. I like it and I'm a good driver. I listen to audio books as I am driving so the journey goes quickly. This looks wonderful Stuart," I say surveying the food. "Now stop worrying and let's eat. I have a few days off next week and that's what so good about this job, it varies so much and I can fit my work in with your shifts."

The simple stir-fry and apple pie is delicious. Afterwards, as we sit comfortably by the fire holding hands with my head on his shoulder, I feel utterly at peace with the world. A glass of wine later he turns, and with those appealing brown eyes looking into mine, he says seriously. "I've changed the bed just in case?"

"Perfect," I say. "I love clean sheets." His eyes light up and he tenderly tips up my chin, looking for confirmation.

"Come," he says as he is reassured that I mean it. He takes my hand and leads me up the stairs.

I am being carried away, his lips are on my face and my neck and I shiver with excitement or fear, I'm not certain which. I close my eyes as he undoes my zip and inserts his hand, stroking my back. I turn sideway so that he can take my dress away from my shoulders. Slowly and carefully, he removes all my clothes. I can feel his fingers trembling and wonder if he too is feeling nervous. Nevertheless he is stroking and caressing me tenderly, trailing his lips and kissing me randomly as he moves. He lifts a questioning eyebrow at my half-grown pubic hair.

"A moment of madness." I smile.

His mouth strays across my knee and then onto my hipbone, onto my wrist, and then he turns my hand and presses his lips to my palm. I giggle and he licks my outstretched fingers. "Are you ticklish Jezebel?" he grins.

All feelings of apprehension disappear as my body responds to his love. I have no feeling of embarrassment as he lays me naked on the bed. Leaning over me he kisses me again, first on my eyelids, then the lobes of my ears and he trails his mouth across my cheek to my lips, his hands tangled in the dark fall of my hair. I am overwhelmed by the feel of him and as my hands explore his back, I become aware of his erection pressing into my thigh.

"You OK?" he asks, his lovely eyes shining.

"Mmm," is all I can manage to reply.

His mouth curves softly and looking down at my body, he says, "Am I allowed to tell you how beautiful you are?"

"You can tell me," I tease him and pull him back toward me. I'm falling completely in love. This isn't just a sexual thrill. I'm giving him myself in a way so different to the others. I know inside my heart that the experience of sex alone without this compelling beautiful feeling is only a temporary thing. We move together so slowly and tenderly, his caresses meaning more to me than the sadistic passion of Ben or the sexual athletics of Tony. Making love to Stuart is like slipping into a warm bath, holding each other with a certainty of comfort and safety. A confirmation of our mutual fondness. It is all I ever wanted, and we murmur to each other as pleasure engulfs us. He coaxes my body skilfully and carefully until we climax together and the earth really does seem to move for me. Perhaps it is my imagination but I really *am* on cloud nine. Here is a man I can truly love. Our love for each other colours the air between us like prism of sunlight.

"I adore you, my little Jezebel," he says. "You know that don't you?"

"I know that at this moment, and I know how I feel about you. It's so special and each day it grows. You make me so happy but I need to know, what is it that makes us so good together?" I ask him when we're curled up next to each other, a bubble of happiness like a beautiful cloud around us.

Stroking my cheek, he says, "OK, let's see… you're not a showy, show-off person, but I think you're smart and clever. I admire you. To me, you're beautiful inside and out, and cool about it." He's obviously taking me seriously. "You don't seem to know how attractive you are without really trying. I like your woolly 'jamas and foxy slippers." He laughs.

"Is that it?" I tease.

"No. I love your body, your face, your voice and I know this is going to sound odd to you, but I think I know your feelings… what you are feeling; happy, sad, insecure. I feel it in my bones, in

179

my very heart sometimes." He takes my hands in his and gently runs his thumbs across the backs of them, bringing a lump to my throat. He raises his head and looks into my face. "Even when you are a 'stroppy mare', I understand and feel your 'feel'."

I put my hand to his face and try to explain why I have reservations. "You have given me so much and I want to believe that our love will go on forever, but I have become so sceptical about long-term relationships. I need to know and understand how to keep these lovely feelings alive and on going. I'm so afraid we will get bored or tired of each other. People do... you see it all the time... moving apart slowly, not watching each other anymore, and love disappears. Do you know when Diane and her husband first came here, they looked like the perfect couple, always holding hands and smiling, facing inwards somehow, towards each other. Brian and I were never like that... but it disappeared and they stopped loving each other… He left with someone else and I saw them together once; Diana's husband and his new love in the post office and they looked just the same. I wonder if they are still 'looking at' each other or whether that too has gone 'stale'."

Stuart turns me towards him and looks at me with those lovely brown eyes that are soft with love and tenderness and says, "I have an idea… We will find a way to keep our feelings fresh and on going. We will make a pact to do at least one thing every month that brings us together, that excites us, that gives us pleasure with each other."

"Like what?"

He puts his hand to his head, "We could be different people, like from a film, Bogart and Bergman, Sharon Stone and Michael Douglas... what was that film? It was very naughty. Or we could have liaisons in unusual places, like the kitchen or on the stairs or we could --"

"Stop, I can't act, and the stairs are out of the question, much too uncomfortable."

"OK, let's make a list of things we would like to do, places and situations, anything exciting and fun, a very long list and we will work through it into our old age." He looked into my eyes asking the question and I think for a moment.

What a great idea. I think but say, "OK, I've never been to Paris or made love in the open air."

"On the list. What about in a hot tub or on the beach like Burt Lancaster and thingy... Who was it rolling in the waves with him?"

"We'll have to be practical and do the most athletic things while we're still young enough." I laugh.

"We could see a film, a play or an opera even and re-enact the raunchy bits."

"Sounds good. What about eating peaches in the bath? I saw that in something once."

"A bit tame."

"We'll learn to massage each other and do the naughty bits."

"Play doctors and nurses."

"Definitely that one, you have a thing about that. Do you know something I don't?" I enquired. "How do you feel about ice? Or what about sex toys?"

"We might not need them," he says with a twinkle. "There's more to you than meets the eye too!"

As we laughed together, he said, "Let's do it, we will get a special book, make a long list and tick things off as we do them."

"We might want to do them more than once. We could give them a star rating."

"Absolutely. We'll keep our relationship interesting and exciting, and never get bored with each other."

So we do just that and find so many silly, fun, fantasy and sexy things that will amuse and excite us, including the ice. The list is enormous and we laugh endlessly as we add things as we think about them. We know that we are be going to Jersey in another week for Tally and Michael's wedding. Tally of course is delighted about Stuart and has already sent him an invitation. I'll also be asking Nick and Paula to include Stuart in their invites and have no problem if Brian and Sophie are there. So, Jersey next week and New York in the summer are planned into our list too.

I reflect on my last year of dates and adventures into my own sexuality. I have learnt that real orgasm is when a man and a woman meet from the whole of their need, desire and affection and take each other to all of their responses, not just the thrill of the physical. After all, we can do that fairly satisfactorily on our own. Bedroom athletics are all very well but give me someone who accepts me, makes me laugh and leaves me feeling delirious with thrilling sensations: it's not how hard they pump, how long they can last, how deep they penetrate but the closeness and intimacy that they bring to the pleasuring of each other that counts. Laughter is so important. If you can't laugh together in the bedroom, life is so dull. A woman would rather be under a man who makes her laugh than with a good-looking sexy bore. I realise how long I have been waiting, not just to hear the words but to feel and be overwhelmed by the giddy sensation of love and desire all mixed together.

The bland greyness of my marriage and my life has all but disappeared. From where once, life was a pleasant monochrome. It is now glorious technicolor.

THE END

52335542R00101

Made in the USA
Charleston, SC
16 February 2016